Bookburner
Book Five in the Library Gate Series
By H. Duke

and
Yulewriter
Book four and a half in the Library Gate Series

Dear reader

Thank you for reading the fifth book in the Pagewalker series. Since you liked it enough to get this far, sign up for my reader group at www.hdukeauthor.com[1]. I regularly host giveaways and send out free stories.

Enjoy the story!

-*H. Duke*

---

1. http://www.hdukeauthor.com

Author's Note: The following story takes place between *Inkcaster* (book four) and *Bookburner* (book five) in the Pagewalker series.
It contains important events you'll want to read before starting *Bookburner,* which is why I included it here—so don't skip it, or you might be confused!
Enjoy the bonus story!
-H.

Yulewriter

"When will she wake up?"

The ICU doctor looked up from the clipboard she'd been writing on. Her face took on that scrunched-brow look of calculated sympathy that April had gotten so used to. She'd dealt with a lot of doctors and nurses since Gram had been admitted the previous week.

One week, the week they were supposed to spend in Europe. It seemed like a lifetime.

"Your grandmother's coma was induced by—"

"Pulmonary distress, I know," April said. She'd heard the phrase spoken aloud two dozen times since the doctors discovered the cancer had spread to Gram's lungs. "But when will she wake up?"

The doctor's tone remained clinical and polite. "We don't know. Her blood-oxygen levels have stabilized since we put her on O2. She should be awake now."

"But she isn't."

"I wish I had an answer. Some people just... stop fighting."

April looked down. It was the response she'd dreaded. She wanted to protest and say that Gram would never stop fighting, not until her last breath. Instead, she remained quiet.

The doctor's voice softened, losing its clinical edge. "Are you all right? Is there someone I can call for you?"

April shook her head. "No. There's no one but me." Gram was the only family she had left. Soon she'd be gone. Maybe already was.

The doctor reached out and gripped April's arm. "Her condition is stable. You should go home and sleep. Eat, shower. She'll be here when you get back."

April didn't respond, and the doctor let her hand fall away. She left without another word.

April appraised the woman dwarfed by the hospital bed. She looked too frail to be Gram, who—even with terminal cancer—had always been vibrant and lively. This woman was just a shell.

Was Gram even still in there, or had she moved on already, a spirit gone to wherever spirits go? Was it like forgetting to turn off the lights when you leave home?

Christmas carols being sung in the lobby drifted in. Christmas was a little more than a week away; Friday was the start of the last weekend before the holiday. It didn't feel like Christmas, though, despite the twelve-inch tree that Gram's friend Rita had erected on the dresser. April hadn't even plugged in the lights.

April's phone buzzed. She glanced down at it. Randall, of course.

You okay? How's your grandmother?

She clicked out of the text, then tapped on the "missed calls" tab, wanting to remove the notification from her home screen. Randall had called several times, and both Becky and Janet had called in the previous week. The Werner Room reference desk number showed up nightly. That would be Dorian. There was another number that she thought might have been Thaddeus; she didn't know for sure, though. She hadn't listened to any of her messages, and now her inbox was full.

Her phone buzzed again, and a second message popped up.

Everything here is covered. Take as much time as you need.

Then, *I wish you'd let us know you're okay.*

Guilt flooded April. Before she could change her mind, she hit the reply button.

I'm fine. Gram hasn't woken up yet.

She hit the send button, then put her phone on silent.

"April? Honey?"

April looked up to see Gram's friend, Rita, standing in the doorway. She cradled a poinsettia in her arms. The red blooms against the dark green leaves and gold foil wrapped around the base were beautiful—but the plant would die soon after the holiday. Poinsettias always did, didn't they?

April shook her head. "I'm fine." She didn't feel much like talking.

Rita set the poinsettia down near the foot-tall tree. She clucked when she saw that the tree's lights weren't plugged in. "What will Doris think when she wakes up and sees this tree isn't plugged in? She always loved the holidays."

"The doctors aren't sure if she's going to wake up. Ever."

"She'll wake up," Rita said. "She wouldn't miss Christmas."

"I wish I could be as sure as you."

Rita was right about one thing—Gram did love Christmas. It was the one time of the year when she'd allow herself to forgo green tea and steel-cut oats and indulge in sweets and unhealthy food. She'd always made the holidays a special time of year for everyone, especially April.

One more reason to be upset. Why did this have to happen now? Gram didn't get to go on her European vacation, and now she wouldn't be able to celebrate her favorite holiday for the last time. It was cruel.

There was movement at the door. A group of people wearing matching green-and-red-plaid scarves and holding booklets of music smiled in at them.

"We're from St. Anne's," one of the singers explained. "Can we sing you a few songs?"

Rita clapped her hands together. "Oh, that would be wonderful. They say that people in comas can still hear. Did you know that?"

The carolers smiled vapidly. They'd go home to their families and their presents and their eggnog and music as though Gram wasn't lying in the hospital bed.

April pulled on her coat. "I have to go home." She registered the look of surprise on Rita's face before pushing past the carolers and rushing down the hallway.

She went home and took a shower, just like the doctor suggested. She stepped out of the bathroom knowing she'd never be able to sleep. The house was oppressively quiet. Had April ever been alone in the house at night before? Not that she could remember...

She grabbed her keys. There was one place she could go.

It was almost a quarter to nine when she pulled into the library parking lot. Strands of white lights outlined the building's eaves and windows. It was the sort of display Gram would have called tasteful. When had they put the display up?

She'd hoped that the other librarians would have been gone by the time she pulled in, but they were just filing out. Damn. Why hadn't she waited a few more minutes, driven a little slower? They'd seen her pull up, so there was nothing for April to do but get out and walk towards them.

"April?" Becky said, Janet right behind her. "What are you doing here?" Then, as though she realized how that sounded, "I'm sorry about your grandmother. That's terrible. And right before your big trip, too."

Janet nodded. "At least you already had the time off from work, right?" then she winced. "Sorry."

"It's okay. Thanks."

"So... why are you here?"

"I thought I'd do some work," April said. "I need something to focus on."

They nodded sympathetically but looked unsure. "When the library's closed?" Janet asked.

"I work under the Werner contract, remember? I have access to the collection at all times."

Becky nodded. "I know. But are you sure you want to be up there all by yourself right now?"

"I just need something to do. It might as well be work."

Janet and Becky looked at each other and slowly began nodding. "Okay," Becky said. "Would you like me to stay? I don't have plans tonight."

April cut her off. "No. You should be with your family."

"Well, if you're sure..."

April felt relieved as they started to walk away, but then Janet turned around.

"Have you seen *A Christmas Carol?*"

"The movie?" April asked.

"Not the movie. The book. The first edition up in the Werner Collection."

"Oh." Duh, of course that was what Janet was talking about. "The last time I saw it it was on the high shelf with the other first editions. Why?"

"People have been asking for it. I thought you'd put it somewhere before you left."

April shook her head. "I didn't."

"Well, if you see it, put it on my desk."

Janet and Becky finally left, and April unlocked the door and headed upstairs.

The Werner Room was empty, the lights off.

"Randall?" April called into the empty stacks. "Thaddeus?"

"April? What are you doing here?"

There was movement, like a hand coming out from behind a curtain to open it—if that curtain were camouflaged look like its immediate surroundings. Thaddeus, Randall, and Rex stepped into view.

"Were you just invisible?" April asked.

Thaddeus nodded, holding up the wand as evidence. "Simple cloaking spell."

"Let's just say that Janet is more diligent about checking the library than you were," Randall explained, referencing the night he'd found out about the gate. He'd hidden in the men's restroom to hide from the cold, where April had failed to check.

They fell into an uncomfortable silence. Randall's face was a mask of worry.

"Just thought I'd come in and do some work," she explained.

"We've been worried about you."

"Didn't you get my text message?"

He nodded. "It was very short."

"Like it said, I'm fine," April made her voice as firm as possible. "In fact, I'm giving you two the night off."

"Night off? But—"

"No buts," April said. "Go home. I'll take care of things here."

"I'm not sure that's a good idea," Randall said.

"Please," April said. "I just need some time to myself to think. To focus on something else."

Randall sighed. "Okay. Anyway, Dorian will be here, so you won't be alone. We managed to erase most of the rot, by the way."

"Can Thaddeus help you like he helps me?" April asked. When the rot had gotten bad, they'd discovered that if Thaddeus and April were holding hands while she touched the ink rot, it would immediately erase all the rot in the entire book. Normally she would have to touch each individual tendril. It was quite a trick.

It seemed so long ago.

Randall shook his head. "We tried. It only works with you."

As they pulled on their coats, Randall said, "I'm thinking about having a little get together this weekend to celebrate the holiday. I'll probably invite a few people from the shelter who haven't had something like that to go to in a while. You're welcome to come. It would get your mind off your grandmother."

"Maybe." She just wanted them to leave.

Randall nodded. "We're a phone call away if you need us."

"I know."

Randall gave her a sympathetic look before he and Thaddeus walked down the staircase. Rex followed behind.

As soon as they left, April walked over to the floor board under which *The Picture of Dorian Gray* was hidden. She pulled the book out and closed it.

"Sorry." She wasn't sure if Dorian would even notice that the gate wasn't opening on time. But she needed to be alone.

She put his book back beneath the floor boards. There were a few minutes left before the gate would normally be scheduled to open. She'd find a book with some ink rot and take care of it. At least it was something to do.

The she remembered that she didn't have her Pagewalker powers anymore; Randall did. She couldn't erase any ink rot. *Damn it.* She'd really wanted something to do, something that would keep her mind off Gram and Christmas.

She sighed. Looked like she'd be spending the night actually doing library work.

She'd booted up the computer in her office when the grandfather clock began to chime. *Not tonight,* she thought at it. Her desktop appeared on the screen just as the last tone rang out. She began clicking through her email.

After ten minutes she began to feel cold, even through her sweatshirt. Had someone left a window open? Barb would have a field day. What if the collection got wet?

She walked out into the stacks, looking for the open window, but they were all closed. But there was a breeze, wasn't there, and the high-pitched cry of winter wind, which was weird since there hadn't been a noticeable wind when she'd been outside.

The gate whispered in her ear. Was it possible that a book had been left open somewhere? She checked for opened books throughout her shift, but had never had one left open after hours, at least since Andre died. She figured that Dorian's book would block them anyway, but she wanted to be safe.

"Damn."

She walked around one of the stacks, and sure enough the gate was open to a London street—nineteenth-century, by the looks of it. Mounds of snow mounded the street corners, and fat flakes drifted down from the sky. White drifts had begun to form on the library-side of the gate.

Was *The Picture of Dorian Gray* open? Had she somehow caused the pages to fall open when she replaced the floor board? She didn't think so—not to mention that she was sure no scene from Dorian's book featured snow—but she decided to go check, anyway.

She pulled open the floor board, but Dorian's book was still closed. That meant there was a book open elsewhere in the library.

She replaced the floor board and began checking the study tables. All clear. She moved on to the stands between the armchairs, and the coffee table in the sitting area. Nothing.

She needed to find that book. Well, she'd wanted a distraction, hadn't she? Seemed like she'd gotten one.

She paused between the rows of bookshelves so that she could look down the aisles between them. On the other end, something moved—a figure dressed all in white.

She suppressed a scream, and her heart suddenly threatened to beat right through her ribcage. She'd been sure she was alone.

"Randall?" she called. "Thaddeus? Becky?" She followed the figure, which had moved towards the defunct fireplace. A glowing light was coming from around the shelves.

A spicy scent tickled her nose—evergreen boughs. What was going on?

When she rounded the corner, she stopped in her tracks. The library had changed as she'd followed the figure through the stacks—or had she simply not noticed the fresh garlands hanging from the windows and the ends of every bookcase? Or the lighted candles in each of the windows? Why would anyone light candles in a place filled with flammable and valuable things?

The sturdy plastic chairs and vinyl couch were gone, replaced with a single leather armchair. A small table sat to its right; on it rested a steaming cup and a book with the ribbon inside as though its reader had stepped away for a moment and would be returning shortly.

A fire blazed in the fireplace, its radiant warmth fighting the chill coming through the open gate.

The figure stood in front of the fire. Its head was surrounded by a halo of light so brilliant that it obscured its features. Even though she couldn't see the person's face, she could tell by its silhouette that it was a child. A familiar-looking child.

The brightness dimmed momentarily, revealing dark, wavy hair, brown eyes, and tanned skin.

"Rico?" she said. "What are you doing here?"

The boy didn't nod or shake his head, but said only, "I am the Ghost of Christmas Past."

April placed her hand on her hip. "Is this a joke? Are you in town visiting your grandma or something?"

Rico tilted his head slightly to one side but didn't respond.

"Look," April said. "I haven't read *A Christmas Carol* yet, but I've seen enough movie adaptations to know that the Ghost of Christmas Past doesn't turn into a Latino kid."

Rico tilted his head. "I take whatever form is necessary."

April thought for a moment. Janet *had* said that *A Christmas Carol* had gone missing. Funny enough, it was more likely that the figure standing in front of her was the Ghost of Christmas Past than Rico.

She sighed. "You've got the wrong person. You're supposed to visit Scrooge tonight, not me."

"There is time to help more than one tonight." The spirit looked at the grandfather clock. Fifteen past nine. In *A Christmas Carol,* the first spirit doesn't visit Scrooge until midnight—or at least that was how it had been in the movie adaptations. She'd learned not to trust those as a source of what happens in a book.

She heard voices behind her, as though from a party. They were happy and merry, and the higher tones of excited children were interspersed with the mezzo tones of adults.

She turned to look for the source of the sound, but the library was dark and lifeless.

"Walk with me."

She turned back and jumped. The spirit had moved forward while her head was turned. He now stood in front of her, hand outstretched, fingertips less than a foot away.

She didn't know why, perhaps it was an automatic reaction, or because she couldn't say no to Rico, even someone who was only wearing Rico's face. She reached out and took the spirit's hand.

Nothing happened. The spirit turned so that they both faced the fireplace and the cozy scene surrounding it. The voices behind her grew so loud that she was sure if she just turned around she'd see a roomful of happy people. Before she could look, the spirit pulled her forward.

And then they were in the night sky above Minneapolis.

"Ahh!" April kicked reactively. She clutched the spirit's hand, sure he was the only thing keeping her from plummeting.

"You won't fall," the spirit said. "Come."

They drifted forward. As April calmed, she recognized the white lights of the library. Every few moments they flickered, and the display would be slightly different; brighter, dimmer, a section of lights dark. The tenth or twelfth time the lights became colored, and soon after that they were replaced with candles on the windowsills—the same style of candle she'd seen inside the Werner Room.

The flickering happened to almost every building they passed over. Some that didn't have displays suddenly had them, or the lights would change in color, intensity, or placement.

As they flew past some of these flickering displays, April recognized the route: They were heading to April and Gram's house.

"No one's there," April said.

"Not now," the spirit agreed, but they continued moving anyways.

Soon their house came into view. Of course, it had no Christmas lights—but then it did, and April recognized the lights they'd put up last year, only on the bushes in front, the places they wouldn't need a ladder to get to. Then the house flickered again, and lights were added to the gutters. The display remained the same for the next several flickers, with minor differences—a strand out here, a window cling there.

Then Gram's beloved white lights were replaced by colored strands.

"These are the lights Gram used to put up when I was a kid," April said, drinking in the vision, her heart suddenly filled with a not unpleasant weight. "But she hates colored lights."

When April looked over, the spirit's face was again obscured by the halo of blinding light. The light dimmed and brightened like the flame of a candle, though much brighter. Sometimes she could just make out the shape of Rico's features. Then they'd be drowned out by the light again.

"Then why did she hang these?"

"Your father loved them."

"Oh. She hung them even after he died."

"She hung them until they no longer worked," the spirit said.

Before April could ask more, she noticed that they were getting very close to the front window of the house and weren't slowing down.

"We're going to crash!" April braced for the impact, but none came. When she opened her eyes they were landing in Gram's old living room. The spirit peered at her, though his gaze wasn't worried or even amused. Or maybe the flame in front of his face obscured his expressions.

Wanting to break the gaze, April turned to look around the living room. "Everything's different," she said. "The coffee table is in the wrong spot, and I've never even seen that couch..."

A Christmas tree stood against the wall adjacent to the television stand. The television was boxy and probably weighed more than she did. She recognized many of the ornaments, but there were several that she didn't recognize.

Beneath the tree was a child, no older than three. The child lay on her back, staring up through the branches at the glowing lights, laughing.

"I used to do that," April said.

"You did that even last year," the spirit reminded her.

April nodded, too awestruck to feel sheepish about the admission. It was true—she loved looking up through the branches at the blinking lights and reflective orbs. It was like a kaleidoscope of color, never quite the same yet familiar and comforting.

April examined the child, and realized she'd seen those candy cane-striped pajamas in Gram's photo albums. "That's me?" she asked.

"Yes."

"Then this is—"

"The first Christmas after your parents' accident," the spirit finished.

Footsteps approached. April looked up to see Gram hurrying towards the living room.

"April!" Gram exclaimed. "You have to stay in your crib. You could get hurt out here by yourself."

Gram's tone was more worried than mad, and pint-sized April didn't seem admonished at all. She laughed and pointed at the tree. "Santa?" she said.

"Yes, Santa comes tomorrow night—if you're a good girl and stay in your crib. Santa only visits good girls and boys, remember?"

April's tiny face became serious. She nodded. "I stay."

"Good girl."

Gram carried her back to her room. April and the spirit followed, watching Gram tuck the younger version of herself into bed.

"Gram?" Baby April said.

"Yes, hon?"

"April good, Santa bring Mommy and Daddy?"

Gram's face twisted, and her eyes became misty. She forced her mouth to form a small smile. "That's not the kind of thing Santa does. I wish it was."

April looked disappointed. "Okay."

"But Santa will bring you everything else you asked for—if you're good and go to sleep! Got it?"

Tiny April's face twisted into a large grin. "Uh-huh!" How easy it was for her to forget.

"Good girl."

Gram walked out the room and closed the door. April worried a moment about being trapped inside with her younger self, but the spirit stepped through the wall without thought. April followed, surprised to feel nothing as she passed through the painted plaster.

Gram's door, directly across the hall, clicked closed, a light appearing underneath the door. Muffled sobbing penetrated it.

April walked through the door. Gram sat on the edge of her bed, her hand pressed to her mouth, quieting her cries so that tiny April wouldn't hear. She reached over to her bedside table and picked up a framed photograph. April recognized the picture—it was of her parents, taken the year before April was born. They stood in front of a mountain somewhere, grinning widely.

"It's okay, Gram," April said. She tried to touch Gram's shoulder, but her hand just passed through her.

"She can't hear you or feel you," the spirit said.

April nodded. She'd known this, of course, but couldn't stand seeing Gram that way. How much pain Gram must have gone through to give April a good Christmas? April felt a pang of guilt.

The scene melted. April and the spirit stood in a crowded café. Despite the outdated furniture, April recognized it as the restaurant Gram and Rita would meet at every week or so.

"I don't think I can stand it, Rita. How do I get through the holidays without my son? This was always his favorite time of year."

April turned at the sound of Gram's voice. She and Rita sat at the table behind them. Gram clutched a mug of coffee in one hand—*Gram used to drink coffee?*—a panini with two bites taken out of it rested in the table in front of her, the melted cheese already congealed.

Rita reach out and placed a hand on Gram's arm. "You have to, Doris, for—"

"For April's sake, I know," Gram finished dully. "The poor child doesn't even understand what's happened. Sometimes I think she's figured it out, but then she'll ask me when Mommy and Daddy are coming back."

"She's too young to process it." Rita took a sip of her own coffee. "Yes, you need to do it for April, but you also need to do it for yourself. You have to enjoy things. John would want you to. You have to heal. You have to keep living."

Gram thought for a long time, staring down at the panini intensely, as though it might know the solution to the conundrum.

She sighed. "You're right. I have to do it for April. But I don't think I'll ever really enjoy Christmas again. How can I?"

"You will." Rita patted her arm. "I think you're making the right decision. And I bet you'll be glad you did. I can come over and help you with the lights..."

April shook her head. "Rita was wrong. Gram was crying because Christmas reminded her of my dad. It must have been so painful for her to pretend to be happy."

"In a way it was," the spirit said. "But you're wrong about why she was crying. Did you know that your father used to lie under the Christmas tree just like you do when he was younger?"

April shook her head.

"That's the reason you snuck out to do it. Your father did that with you the previous year. Gram saw you lying there and remembered her son, your father, and was comforted. Those were tears of sadness, yes, but also tears of joy and healing."

April couldn't quite believe this, but in the recesses of her memory, she thought she remembered the feeling of a strong, protective presence lying with her underneath the tree. It was partially why she found it so comforting. Was it possible that was her dad? Or a memory of him, at least? She'd always assumed she didn't have any memories of him, except the stories Gram had told her.

The scene dissolved, becoming darker. The sour odor of trash filled the air. They had reappeared underneath a bridge. People dressed in thick, bulky layers of mismatched clothing huddled in groups. Some were pressed against the far wall, hiding from the wind; others crowded around trash can fires, raising their hands to the flames. Fat flakes of snow fell around them, collecting on top of their hats and hoods like icing sugar. They didn't seem to notice.

"Where are we?" April asked.

The spirit didn't respond. She turned to look at him. The halo had dimmed again, perhaps so that she wouldn't get distracted by it in the darkness.

Rico's face had begun to stretch, grow older. He had also grown several inches, and his waist had expanded.

"What's happening to you?" April asked.

"My time grows short," the spirit said, then nodded toward two figures, one human, wrapped in several layers of winter clothing. A dog slept next to him, everything but his face covered by blankets.

"Rex?" April stepped towards the figures. The dog lifted its head—confirming that it was Rex. For a second April thought he saw her. Then the dog lowered its head again, tucking it beneath the thigh of the man sitting next to him.

Randall. He fiddled with a small evergreen branch, trying to get it to stand up by inserting it into a tin can filled with rocks. It fell over twice more before finally remaining upright. Then he pulled a handful of objects from a plastic bag at his side. Earrings, pieces of tinfoil, and other small trinkets. He hung these from the branch, one by one.

Satisfied, he reached inside his coat, grimacing as he worked his hand through the layers, before pulling out two pictures. April leaned in close to see them. One was of an attractive dark-skinned woman, the other a smiling girl. April recognized Randall's deep brown eyes in the girl's face.

The pictures were bent and cracked. Randall set them up against the edge of the can.

"Merry Christmas, girls." He lay down on his side facing them. He began to pull another comforter over him and Rex, but footsteps approached. Randall's face hardened.

A young figure with a mean, rat-like face appeared. He appeared eighteen, maybe twenty. Rex growled.

"Rex," Randall admonished, and the dog fell silent.

"Setting up a little Christmas tree, Washington?" the kid said, his voice both angry and mocking. "Christmas doesn't come here."

With that, the kid kicked the can, sending the tree—and Randall's pictures—flying. The kid stalked back to the group near one of the fires and Randall hurried after the mess, picking up the photos first, checking each one and brushing them off before returning them to his pocket.

He collected his ornaments and reassembled the tree as best he could. It now looked a little lopsided, and many of the needles that had been clinging to it now littered the ground.

"Don't worry about him, Rex," Randall said. "He's had a hard life. Poor kid. No, don't worry about him at all..."

He started muttering to himself, reminding April of how he'd been when she'd first started working at the library. He'd been more unstable then, more volatile. He'd become such a support for her that she'd forgotten how much he'd changed.

He didn't put the photos out again. He pulled the comforter over him and Rex. They fell still.

"He could freeze to death," April said. "It can go fifty degrees below zero in the city." She couldn't feel the chill on her skin, but she could see the thick clouds of steam escaping from the homeless people's mouths.

"He could have," the spirit agreed. "But he didn't."

The underpass disappeared, replaced by the library. The fire had begun to die down. The book was gone and only dregs remained in the bottom of the cup. The spirit stood behind her, and the flickering light from his halo dimmed.

It was no longer Rico standing there, but Andre, the same as the last day she'd seen him.

"My time is up," the spirit said, not offering an explanation for the change. "The next spirit will arrive at the chiming of the bell."

April opened her mouth to ask what she was supposed to learn from what she'd seen—she was supposed to learn something, right? Wasn't that that point?—but the halo around the spirit's head grew so bright that she had to shield her eyes. It exploded like a supernova, turning everything white...

Then the library was dark.

She blinked as her eyes adjusted. "Spirit?" she asked. "Are you all right?"

But he was gone. The fire was out, too, not even a scorch mark on the hearth to prove that it had been there at all. The armchair had likewise disappeared.

If she didn't know better, she would have thought that she'd hallucinated the encounter. But with the gate around, that wasn't likely.

She looked at the clock—nine forty-five. "I have to find that book," she said out loud. She wasn't in the mood for another preachy spirit session. She had fifteen minutes. It had to be somewhere.

She searched for over ten minutes, even bending down to peer beneath the tables to see if someone had left it on the seat of one of the chairs. Desperate, she started pushing back the books on the shelves so she could look at the space between them and those on the adjoining shelf. She did find one book resting open on its spine. She gripped at it excitedly, but it turned out to be a copy of *Fifty Shades of Gray*.

"Ugh!" She moaned, frustrated.

She went to go check the next shelf, but halfway there the clock began to tick. She winced. Too late...

She counted out the strokes. When the tenth echoed out into the library, she glanced around, waiting for the next spirit to make its entrance. But none appeared.

The library remained silent. Was it possible that they'd given up? Maybe they'd figured out that she wasn't who they were supposed to be helping tonight...

Just when she allowed herself to start believing it, a feminine voice echoed up from the stairwell. She couldn't make out what it was saying, but it had a lilting quality to them that was almost soothing.

She followed the voice down the stairs, knowing that ignoring it would do no good. She didn't have time for this. She needed to find the book and close it...

The air was filled with the tempting scent of cinnamon sugar and baking dough. The voice got clearer the farther down the stairs she got. When she reached the bottom she realized that it wasn't speaking, but singing:

"*God rest ye merry gentlemen and maids upon this day...*"

She recognized first the song, then the voice.

"Rita?" She turned the corner into the break room. Almost every surface was covered in racks of cooling cookies, and those that weren't held platters of mouthwatering baked goods. There was every kind of Christmas treat you could imagine; chocolate chip, iced sugar, ginger bread, several different varieties of fudge, and more that April couldn't even name.

Rita leaned over the open oven. Like the upstairs fireplace it hadn't been used since the kitchen had been repurposed as a break room; yet Rita—clad in a red apron and green oven mitts—pulled a steaming tray out of the oven.

She turned around, her face melting into a look of delight. "April! What a pleasant surprise!"

"You weren't expecting me?"

"You weren't exactly on our list of cases for the night." Her face shifted into an expression of indulgent admonishment. "But Past is so sentimental. They couldn't leave you to your suffering after seeing how unhappy you were."

"I'm fine, really," April said, seeing an opportunity to possibly talk herself out of all of this. "You don't need to—"

"Don't lie to me, dear," the spirit said, her wrinkled face stern. "I've known you your entire life, after all."

"You're not really Rita."

"Of course I'm not—though as far as you're concerned I might as well be—but that doesn't mean I haven't *known* you." She busied herself with the cookies, looking for a place to set the hot tray. "Do you mind, dear?" she nodded towards a spatula.

April grabbed the spatula and began shifting room-temperature cookies from one of the cooling racks and onto a serving platter. Then she carefully began peeling the cookies off the tray in the spirit's hands onto the newly empty rack.

"We used to do this when I was younger," April said. "You, me, and Gram spent a whole Saturday every December baking cookies."

"Did we?" the spirit said. "I wouldn't know. That's Past's expertise." She nodded to the cooling rack. "Try one. They're best when they're nice and hot."

April carefully lifted the still-gooey cookie off the rack. It melted in her mouth, not quite hot enough to burn her tongue. "Peanut butter," April said, then covered her mouth—Rita hated it when people talked with their mouths full.

"How is it?"

"Delicious. Aren't you going to have one?"

Rita smiled. "No, dear."

"Watching your figure?" April remarked with a raised eyebrow.

The spirit smiled. "Something like that."

April was just about to ask her why the spirit would turn up as her grandmother's best friend when a buzzer sounded on the stove.

"Almost ready..." the spirit said, even though she'd just pulled the cookies out of the oven. April was sure she hadn't seen her put another batch in.

"What's—" April started, but before she could finish, the break room around them dissolved. They were in a dark apartment.

"This is Thaddeus and Randall's apartment," April said, recognizing the open kitchen and the scribbles on the wall. It seemed that Randall had gotten tired of Thaddeus' madness-fueled wall-scribbling, so he'd plastered every wall of the apartment with long sheets of butcher paper. Many of these were covered in Thaddeus' tight scrawl, but not all. Thaddeus had been having fewer episodes lately. Some were connected with long strands of colored yarn. It looked like the wall of a detective trying to solve a case.

Randall sat at the breakfast bar worrying a letter-sized piece of paper in his hands. The paper was folded in half.

Before April could look at the paper, Thaddeus walked into the living room.

"Hey," Randall said, turning the paper over.

"Good evening." Thaddeus nodded at the thing in Randall's hand. "What's that?"

Randall reluctantly flipped over the paper, revealing a picture of two smiling faces, older versions of the woman and girl he'd had pictures of underneath the bridge.

"My wife and daughter," Randall explained. "Found it on Facebook. They were baking Christmas cookies. At least that's what the description said." He smiled. "I'd tell my daughter to change her privacy settings if things were better between us."

"You could go see them," Thaddeus said. "They live in the city, right?"

Randall shook his head. "I tried once. It didn't work out. I don't want to complicate their lives more than I already have. And now my daughter thinks I only show up when I need something. It's better if I stay away. She has a family of her own now. Who wants to tell their kids their grandfather's a bum?"

Thaddeus raised an eyebrow. "You've got a place to live and a sort of volunteer position at the library. I don't think you can call yourself a bum anymore."

Randall snorted, but didn't respond to the comment. "What about you? Do you have family?"

"No. My father's been dead for nearly a decade, and he was all I ever had."

Randall nodded, carefully folding the picture and tucking it into his wallet. "About this party..."

Thaddeus glanced dubiously at the walls of the apartment. "Do you really think having a party here is a good idea?"

Randall shrugged. "The guys wouldn't bat an eye at this, trust me. They've seen it all." He paused. "But you're right. I don't know why I even came up with it in the first place." He remained silent for nearly a minute, then tucked the photo into his pocket. "I'll let the guys know tomorrow that it's cancelled. I'm going to bed."

He stood and walked back down the hallway and disappeared behind the door opposite the one that Thaddeus had come out of earlier.

"That's good," April said to herself. "I don't think a party would have worked out. No one's in the mood to celebrate."

Rita's voice came from April's elbow. "Sometimes you have to fake it until you make it, dear."

April watched Thaddeus at the bar. He glanced up at one section of scribbles on the wall and shook his head in disgust. "Christmas used to be so easy," she muttered. "Now it just makes things so hard."

Rita laughed. "Easy? That's a child's Christmas. Parents and loved ones always work so hard to ensure their sons and daughters have the best holidays possible. The responsibility falls to us as we get older. Both for ourselves and others."

The timer rang again. The apartment dissolved, replaced by Gram's hospital room. The puff and whir of the oxygen tank was punctuated by the slow-but-steady beep of the heart rate monitor.

"Rita went home about an hour ago," the spirit said from over her shoulder.

"She's so alone," April said. In spite of herself, April felt thankful for the Christmas tree still glowing on the dresser. Its soft, comforting light made the room feel less empty. If Gram woke now, it would be the first thing she saw.

"We're all alone, aren't we?" the spirit mused.

"I shouldn't have left her. I should be there now."

The spirit clucked, a sound the real Rita often made. "Now, making yourself sick won't do anything for your grandmother. You need to take care of yourself as much as you need to take care of her."

The timer rang again. "Just enough time for one last stop," the spirit said, and Gram's hospital room dissolved into dark mahogany. A fire blazed in the fire place. Dorian's study.

He stood at the far window, gazing at the street below. His mouth pressed into a thin, worried line.

He looked at a door in the opposite side of the wall. Judging by the angle it was where the gate materialized.

Dorian began to pace. April winced—that answered the question of whether or not he knew that the gate hadn't opened on time.

"He's worried for you," the spirit said.

"I know."

The timer went off once again, and the ticking stopped.

"Time's up," the spirit said, and Dorian's study dissolved. They were back in the break room. All the cookies were gone, as though greedy, unseen hands had come and eaten them. Now only crumbs remained.

"All your hard work," April said, gesturing towards the empty platters.

The spirit clucked again. "The point wasn't the cookies themselves, dear. It was the enjoyment they bring, the connection. Such pleasures are fleeting, but that doesn't mean the work that went into them wasn't worthwhile." The spirit wrapped her arms around April. "You'll understand soon enough."

"What happens now?" April asked. Panic rose in her chest. She dreaded what she was sure would come next.

"Future," the spirit said, her voice distant. And then she was gone. April glanced around her. The cookies, trays, and cooling racks had faded, leaving no trace of the spirit's presence.

April turned towards the stairwell. She had to find that book. She already knew what the future held—a grave. And in the original story it might be Scrooge's grave, but April was sure the one she was about to see wouldn't be her own.

She took the stairs two at a time. The clock began to ring as her feet fell on the first step. The tenth ring had already sounded when she reached the top of the landing. The last came as she stepped through the double doors.

Nothing happened, but she knew better than to assume she was in the clear. She still had to find the book. She hadn't checked her desk yet; what if some hapless volunteer had placed it there?

She entered her office, pulling up the papers and books that had piled up in her absence. Nothing.

Voices out in the library caught her attention. Male, familiar. At least two of them.

"She's not ready to come back." This voice belonged to Randall.

April followed the voices. She darted through the shelves, emerging next to the east wall. The gate was open to Dorian's study. He, Randall, and Thaddeus sat around one of the study tables.

"Can you blame her after what's happened?" Dorian said.

"What's happened?" she asked. Her heart hammered in her chest.

No one turned towards her. How had they gotten here, anyway? Dorian should still be in his study waiting for the gate to open, and Randall and Thaddeus had been in their apartments only minutes before.

Rex whined, looking at her. Or was he looking behind her?

Randall nodded. "There's no doubt that she needs more time, but she shouldn't be left alone right now."

"It's a shame about her grandmother." Thaddeus shook his head.

"Gram?" April said. "What's happened to Gram?" No one answered, and she was almost glad for it. She knew, anyway. Gram had months left at the most. This was Christmas future, and there was no way Gram had made it to next Christmas—it was possible that she hadn't even made it to *this* Christmas.

A figure cloaked in black approached her from behind. The Ghost of Christmas Future. Behind the figure was vast darkness, even though April had just come from that direction; there was no sense of the library there at all, only endless, murky black.

"Why show me this if there's no way I can change it?" April said, anger filling her chest. "Gram's going to die by next year, anyway—why put me through this?"

The spirit didn't answer. It raised an arm and pointed—the sleeves were so long that the fabric draped down over the outstretched finger.

Even before she looked, April heard the puff and whirr of oxygen, and the all-too-familiar beeping. She turned back. The library had been replaced by Gram's hospital room. Gram was still in her bed. She was alive next Christmas? That was impossible.

Movement in the far corner drew April's attention. She looked over to see herself sleeping in the armchair, arms crossed over her chest, a pained look on her face. Her brow furrowed but she didn't rise from her sleep, only turned so that she faced the opposite way.

Rita's Christmas tree remained on the dresser. It wasn't plugged in. The sound of laughter and music drifted down the hallway towards them, but barely penetrated the sad, dark space.

April glanced down at the clipboard hanging off the end of the hospital bed.

"December twenty-fourth," she read. "Christmas Eve."

"Some Christmas."

April turned towards the spirit, gasping as the figure reached up and lowered the black hood.

April recognized the curled white hair, the sparkling blue eyes. They were the same as those of the woman lying in the bed.

"Gram?"

The spirit smiled sadly. "No, hon. I'm not your grandmother."

April nodded, blinking back the tears. "Of course not." She turned back to the woman in the bed. "I thought..."

"That I'd show you your grandmother's grave? No. Such harsh treatment is reserved for only the most advanced lack of Christmas spirit. That's not you. Not yet."

"I thought you'd show me next year's Christmas," April said. "That's what you did in *A Christmas*—I mean, that's what you're going to show Scrooge."

"It's not next year's Christmas that's at stake."

April waited for several moments, afraid to ask the next question. The spirit waited, and April got the distinct impression that it knew what April was working up the courage to ask.

"Is there a way to save her?" The words tumbled out of April's mouth.

The spirit shook its head sadly. "I'm afraid not. This will be your grandmother's last Christmas."

April's vision was momentarily blurred. "Then why show me this? Why show me if I can't do anything to stop it? Scrooge gets to change his fate! Why can't I?"

"I never said you couldn't change anything." The spirit nodded to the room. "Look. What's wrong with this scene?"

"Gram's in a coma, obviously."

"Besides that. *Look.*"

April looked around the room, trying not to linger on Gram's too-small form. The place was dark, quiet. It was as though it ate the warm glow of the lights and laughter from the rooms across the hall.

"She's alone," April said finally.

The spirit nodded. "She is. And so are you."

Somewhere distant, a clock began to chime. "What do I do?" April asked, panic filling her heart. Their time was up and she felt like she hadn't learned anything.

"You already know that." the spirit began to fade.

"No, I don't. Gram? Come back!"

But the spirit was gone, and April was back in the library. The gate was still open to a scene from *A Christmas Carol*. A small boy carrying what looked like a pheasant on his back ran across the street. He looked so happy, so carefree.

April stood for several moments. The tree in the corner twinkled. April walked over to it, bending down so that she could see underneath it. There it was—*A Christmas Carol,* open on the floor. Some kid must have brought it there. It was open to a beautifully illustrated page.

April closed it. Janet would be relieved. She placed a sticky note on the cover and set it on the reference desk for her to find when she came in in the morning.

What now?

You know what to do.

April walked over to the floor board where Dorian's book was hidden. She pulled it up, then opened his book. The gate opened, and by the time it had opened all the way he was standing on the other side.

"What happened?" he said. "Did the Collectors—"

April shook her head. "It wasn't them. I... needed some time to think."

Dorian's eyes widened. "You're supposed to be with your grandmother. Where are Randall and Thaddeus?"

"I sent them home. I think I know what needs to be done now."

"You do?"

She nodded. "I think so. Will you come with me?"

Dorian looked confused, but then nodded. "Okay. Whatever you need."

As they left he caught sight of *A Christmas Carol* sitting on the reference desk. "You didn't go in there, did you? You have to be careful of those spirits. They're quite meddlesome."

April couldn't help but smile.

~~~

They picked up Randall, Thaddeus, and Rex. Everyone's questions about where they were going quieted as they approached the hospital.

No one spoke as they rode the elevator up to Gram's floor. It took some time to convince the nurse at the desk to allow them to see Gram outside of visiting hours, but finally she relented, saying, "If anyone asks, you're all family." April got the feeling she had more important things to deal with.

They sat stiffly in Gram's room for several minutes. Everyone kept glancing at April, looking to her on how to act. She just shrugged. She wasn't sure, either.

She turned toward Rita's dark tree. She stood and flicked the switch to turn on the lights. The room immediately became lighter, less sad.

"My daughter used to have one of these little trees in her room when she was younger," Thaddeus remarked. "She loves Christmas trees. I do, too."

April nodded. "I used to lie underneath the tree branches and look up at all the lights and baubles shimmering through the green needles."

Dorian smiled. "We never had our trees up for this long—and we used real candles on the branches, if you can believe it. Nearly set the house on fire a time or two."

Thaddeus shook his head. "We never had Christmas trees when I was growing up." Then his face softened. "But my dad would cook Christmas breakfast. He was a good cook, my father, if you can believe it..."

They spoke, one after another, recounting Christmas memories and jokes. Soon everyone was laughing and speaking so loudly that the nurse popped in.

"Don't make me regret letting you up here," she said.

"We'll keep it down," April promised. "Sorry."

The nurse's features softened. "Just keep the door closed so that you don't disturb the other patients. Believe it or not, most people are asleep at this hour."

She left and they continued to talk. Finally everyone fell silent.

"Why did you bring all of us here?" Randall asked. "Don't get me wrong, I'm glad. But..." he trailed off.

"This is Gram's last Christmas," April said. "I want to make it the best one possible. Even if she doesn't remember it, I will."

Everyone fell silent. They listened to the beeping and puffing and whirring of the machines that monitored Gram's lifesigns.

April looked up, her brow furrowed. Had Gram's heartrate gotten faster?

She turned to Gram. Her eyelids were fluttering.

"Gram?" April said, nearly breathless. "Gram? Can you hear me?" She took Gram's hand and squeezed it—and Gram squeezed back.

She moaned, then said, "I heard people talking... a party..." she blinked, looking around the room. "Who are your friends, dear?" Her voice sounded froggy, and Randall quickly grabbed a water bottle and straw and held it to her lips. She drank gratefully.

"Hello, Randall," she said to him after she'd finished. "It's nice to see you again." She shifted her gaze to Thaddeus and Dorian. "And who are you two?"

"Gram, this is Thaddeus."

Thaddeus inclined his head. "A pleasure to meet you."

Gram furrowed her brow. "Have we met before? I swear I've heard your voice."

Thaddeus shrugged, looking at April for direction. She wasn't ready to explain everything, so she turned to Dorian. "This is Dorian."

Gram's brow furrowed again. "Dorian? And we *haven't* met before?"

"We haven't," Dorian said. "But it's a real pleasure. April talks about you all the time."

Gram looked at April. "Dorian's a popular name these days." She shook her head. "I'm sorry. Not a lot's making sense right now. What happened?"

April winced. "You passed out while we were packing, Gram," April said.

Gram sat up but then winced. "I did? You mean we missed the trip?"

April nodded. "I'm afraid so."

"How long?" Gram said. She glanced over at the tree. "Did I miss Christmas?"

"No. But Gram, you've been in a coma. For a week!"

Gram lowered herself back down. "Good."

A nurse popped her head in the room. "Is everything all right? We got a spike on the heart-rate monitor—" she stopped when she saw that Gram was awake, then went back out into the hallway to call the other nurses. A minute later they were being pushed out of the room.

"I don't know what you did," the nurse said, "but somehow it drew your grandmother out of her coma." She paused. "Come back during normal visitor hours—and bring your friends."

"I will," April said.

~~~

Gram came home from the hospital on Saturday. It was already dark when they pulled up in front of the house.

"Why, it looks wonderful," Gram said when she saw the twinkling white lights on the bushes. "Did you do all this?"

April grinned. "With some help."

Gram glanced around at the street. "And what are all these cars doing here?"

"I thought we'd have a little welcome-home-slash-Christmas party," April said. "Is that okay? If you're too tired—"

"I slept for seven days. I think it's a great idea."

They were greeted by carols blaring from the stereo. Rita had done a fine job erecting the Christmas tree with Randall and Thaddeus' help. She was now in the kitchen baking as she chatted with Gram's friends from the gym. A few men were talking with Randall—he'd asked shyly if he could invite some of his friends from the shelter.

"The more, the merrier," she'd responded.

Everyone cheered when Gram entered the house. Gram spent the next hour or so greeting guests. Still weak, she spent most of that time on the couch. Attendees stopped to wish her well and say merry Christmas.

The hospital had given them the number of an oxygen machine dealer. Gram wouldn't need it all the time, at least not at first, but they had to make arrangements now so she'd have it when she did need it. The doctors had predicted Gram's condition would improve—in the short term.

But they'd think about that after the holiday. Today, they were celebrating with friends and family.

When the flow of well-wishers slowed, Gram turned to April. "Where's your other friend? *Dorian*?" She raised an eyebrow, and April's face grew warm. She'd introduced Dorian as himself in the hospital. She'd been so emotional that she'd forgotten she'd also introduced Barty with that name when they were trying to convince Gram he was her boyfriend. If Gram had noticed, she hadn't mentioned the inconsistency, but April was sure that wouldn't last long.

"We'll see him soon. Do you like the party?"

Gram covered April's hand with her own. "It's perfect. Exactly how I would want things to be." Moisture gathered at the corners of her eyes. April hoped they were tears of happiness.

At fifteen minutes to nine, Randall looked at April, his eyebrows raised. "Are you sure you want to do this?"

April nodded.

She walked over to Gram, who was laughing with Rita.

"This is a wonderful party," Rita told April.

"I couldn't have pulled it off without you," April said.

Rita smiled humbly. "I was happy to help, though I was surprised when you called me. You didn't seem to be in the holiday spirit."

"I wasn't," April said, "but something changed, I guess."

Rita's squeezed her hand. "I'm glad it did."

April smiled. "Me, too." She turned to Gram. "Listen—there's something I have to show you."

"Show me what?" Gram asked, curious. "A Christmas present?"

"Sort of. We have to go out to see it, though."

Gram still looked doubtful, but said, "All right." She turned to Rita. "Think you can keep an eye on things here?"

Rita nodded. "Of course—I can't wait to hear what the big surprise is, myself."

The doctors said Gram could and should walk short distances to keep her lungs as healthy as possible, but they'd sent them home with a loaner wheelchair, just in case. It remained in the trunk of the car, and Gram refused to hear any talk of them running out to get it for her. April took that as a good sign. She helped Gram pull on her coat. Thaddeus and Randall walked down the stairs.

"Ready?" Thaddeus asked.

"You're coming, too?" Gram asked. "This must be some surprise."

"I'll explain everything soon," April promised.

Gram stared out at the Christmas lights as they passed by. Her brow furrowed as they turned into the library parking lot. "The library?" she said. "Isn't it closed?"

April nodded. "It's okay. I have a key."

"Are you sure we're allowed to do this?" Gram asked as April unlocked the library door. She was slightly breathless, but not so badly that she couldn't talk.

"Yeah," April said. "Comes with the gig."

They managed to convince Gram to use the Mae's old chairlift to ascend the stairs. As she slowly rose up on the track, the Werner Room clock began to chime.

Gram noticed April and Randall exchanging glances.

"What?" she asked.

"You'll see."

When Gram reached the top of the stairs, April didn't bother pointing out the electric scooter parked at the top of the landing. She was glad it was there all the same. Someday Gram might need it.

"Are the lights always on in here?" she asked. "They were off when we were in the parking lot." Her eyes widened as Dorian stepped around the edge of a bookshelf. "You're here, too? I didn't see any other cars." She looked up at April. "What's going on?"

April breathed out. "It's best if we show you." They wheeled Gram over towards the eastern wall, but the portal was closed.

"You closed it?" she asked Dorian.

He nodded, handing her his book. "I thought you should do the honors."

"Closed what?" Gram said, her expression growing more and more suspicious. "Is this a joke?"

"It's not. Just watch." She opened *The Picture of Dorian Gray*. The gate opened revealing his study.

Gram's mouth fell open. "What's happening?"

"Gram, this is where Dorian lives." She closed his book and handed it to her. The gate closed.

"*The Picture of Dorian Gray,*" Gram said, her hands moving over the leather cover. "You mean..." she looked up at Dorian, a question in her eyes.

He nodded. "Dorian Gray, at your service."

"You're a... story book character," Gram said, and Dorian nodded. She looked up at Randall and Thaddeus. "And you two...?"

They both shook their heads. "We live down the street."

She nodded, turning back to April. "So this book is connected to the library?"

"Not just this book," April said. She pulled another off the shelf and opened it. The gate opened to reveal a seaport, the waves lapping up against the dock, gray ocean extending off into the distance.

Gram's eyes widened. April understood; it was one thing to see a study connected to the library; the architecture of Dorian's house and the Werner Room weren't that different. But an entire ocean...

Gram turned to April. "Am I dead? Is this the afterlife?" her lip trembled.

"No, Gram," April said. "You're not dead."

She explained everything about the gate, how she'd come to know about it, and her role in guarding it.

She had to give Gram credit. She hardly blinked at the unbelievable things April was telling her. "So that's why you've been coming home so late?"

April nodded.

"Is this why you didn't want to go to Europe?" her lip began to tremble again.

"It's not that I didn't want to go," April said. "I was just worried about leaving the gate unprotected."

"There are a lot of people in many worlds depending on your granddaughter," Dorian said.

Gram looked at him, then back at April. "Why are you showing me this now?"

April glanced at Dorian. He nodded. She turned back to Gram.

"Because with this portal, we can go to Paris, or the Swiss Alps, or Germany. And more. All the places we wanted to go to but never got the chance. I know it's not the same as a European vacation, but..." she trailed off. "What do you think? Will you go with me?"

Gram took a long time to answer. Finally she nodded. "It's not what I imagined, and I'm still not convinced I'm not dead. But... yes. I'll go anywhere with you."

"Great," April said. She gestured to the shelves. "Where to first?"

Bookburner

Book five in the Library Gate Series

Chapter 1

"Are you Randall Washington?"

April looked up from the email she'd been reading on the reference desk computer. Randall was sitting in his usual spot in the armchair nearest the reference desk. In front of him stood Barb, director of library operations for the entire Minneapolis Library System. April hadn't even known Barb was coming in today.

At the last staff meeting Becky, Janet, and the rest of the library staff had proposed offering Randall the vacant nighttime security guard position. April had felt bad that she hadn't been the one to think of it—it was such a good idea—but Barb had said she needed to check with HR. Did this mean...?

Randall's eyes widened. "Yes, ma'am," he said. "Is there a problem?"

"There's a matter I'd like to discuss with you in private," Barb responded. "Would you join me in the conference room?"

Randall looked at Thaddeus, who sat in one of the nearby chairs. Thaddeus shrugged, his eyebrows raised. He, too, was confused.

Randall turned his gaze to April. She nodded, hoping that she looked encouraging. Randall would think that he was in trouble, maybe even that it had to do with the gate. Maybe she should have warned him... but there'd always been the chance that he wouldn't get the job, and she'd wanted to spare him the disappointment.

He broke eye contact, April was sure it was to maintain the image that he and April had no more than the basic librarian-patron relationship.

"Sure." He stood.

"I'll watch your stuff," Thaddeus said, nodding to Randall's backpack.

"Perfect," Barb said. "Follow me."

With one last confused glance at April, Randall followed Barb out into the hallway. Barb didn't blink an eye when Rex followed along behind them. She would have figured out that Randall had a service dog.

Thaddeus walked up to the reference desk. "Do you know what that's about?"

"I think so," April said. "But let's just wait before I tell you, just in case it's not happening, after all."

"Just give me a hint," Thaddeus said. "Is it good or bad?"

Before April could answer, Becky swooped in through the double doors. She ran up to the reference desk.

"I just saw Barb walk up here," she said. "Is it happening?"

"Looks like it," April said. "She took Randall to the conference room."

"Yes!" Becky said. "Janet will be so happy. Randall was such a huge help while you were gone."

"What's happening?" Thaddeus asked, this time directing the question at Becky.

"You're Randall's roommate, right?" Becky said. "I'll let him tell you. It's really his news to tell."

Thaddeus sighed. "Fine." He went and sat back down at the table and picked up the book he'd been reading—*Frankenstein*. Dorian had started him on the same reading list that he'd given April. His eyes weren't moving across the page, though.

"So how's your grandmother?" Becky asked. "I meant to ask earlier but I didn't get the chance."

"She's doing well, all things considered."

April didn't say how well. They'd spent the last two weeks coming to the library after nine, going to a new destination each night. When April was younger, she and Gram had planned out a dream trip across Europe. When the doctors deemed Gram's cancer terminal and her health worsened, it seemed like it would remain a dream. A few days before Christmas April decided to tell Gram about the library gate, the portal that opened to the world of books. They hadn't yet checked off all of the destinations on their list, but they were close.

Every night, Randall and Thaddeus would take Gram home around midnight, and then April and Thaddeus would stay and take care of any remaining ink rot from the outbreak.

Gram had been asleep when April left that morning, unbothered by the whirring sounds made by the new oxygen machine taking up a quarter of her bedroom. April might have been worried if Gram hadn't had a reason for sleeping in. They'd been up late the previous evening visiting Victorian England.

Becky smiled cautiously. "We were all really glad to hear that she woke up, especially with the holiday." She sighed, turning back towards the door Barb and Randall had left through, a disappointed expression on her face. "I suppose

I should head back downstairs. A new *Nerd Journal* book came out this week and it's been bananas."

"I'll phone you as soon as I hear anything," April promised.

Becky nodded and left.

Thirty minutes later—during which April got even less library work done than usual—Barb and Randall reappeared in the hallway. Barb reached out and shook Randall's hand. He accepted the handshake a second too late, a stunned expression on his face.

Barb started down the stairs. Randall watched her for several seconds before walking in towards them. His face was ashen.

April's heart started to beat. Was something wrong? She expected Randall to look happy if he was offered a job. What if HR had found something in Randall's record that made them change their minds, or worse? What if it was so bad that Barb had banned him from the library?

By the time he reached the desk she'd worked herself into a near-panic. Thaddeus appeared next to Randall's elbow. He looked equally worried.

"Well, what'd she say?" April demanded.

"Yeah," Thaddeus echoed. "What did she say?"

Randall paused before answering. "She offered me Andre's old job. I guess some of the night staff have really been pushing for it."

All the tension in April's stomach released. "That's awesome!"

He nodded slightly, more of an automatic response than an actual agreement. "Did you know about this? Was it your idea?"

"I knew about it, but it wasn't my idea. It was Becky and Janet, and, well, pretty much everyone *but* me."

"Oh."

"You don't look very happy," April said, worry creeping back in. "Why don't you look happy? You don't want to work here?"

He rubbed the back of his neck. "It's not that. I just... I already have a job, don't I?"

"You do?"

"Well, yeah. Helping you. Taking the guard job would conflict with that."

April shook her head. "Do you want the job or not? Be honest."

It took Randall a long time to answer. "It's sudden. I never even considered it a possibility that I might work here—you know, the kind of work where you're on a payroll and get benefits. I'm not exactly the most desirable employee. That said, it's a good opportunity. But I wouldn't take it if you didn't want me to," he added quickly. "Everything that's happened in the last few months is because of you. I don't know where I'd be without you."

"It's *not* because of me," April said. "You should take the job."

"Are you sure?"

"I can't think of anyone who deserves it more than you."

Randall's face slowly broke out into a grin. "Okay."

"I'm glad," April said. If they weren't trying to keep up appearances she would have hugged him.

"Me, too," Thaddeus chimed in. "Now you'll finally be able to pay your portion of the rent." Despite the jab, he too, was grinning.

Becky appeared at the top of the stairs. Apparently April had waited too long to call down with an update. "I saw Barb leave," she said. "What happened?"

"She offered me a job," Randall said. "Looks like I'm going to be working with you guys."

"I'm so, *so* happy!" Becky clapped her hands together and bounced on her heels.

"Thanks," Randall said shyly. "What you did... it really means a lot."

"Don't thank me." Becky shrugged. "You're the one who's been doing the job for free for the last few months. A good guard is hard to come by. Did Barb say what happens next?"

"Barb gave me her phone number. I'm supposed to call her when I decide." He paused. "Do you think it makes me sound too eager if I call her back today?"

Becky shook her head. "She'll want to get you started right away—and the next employee orientation is tomorrow! If you miss it, you'll have to wait until next month." She grinned. "I'm going to text Janet. She'll want to know. Yay! We're going to be co-workers!"

She squealed in delight, then hurried towards the stairs, a bounce in her step.

Randall nodded. "I'd better call Barb. I'll be in one of the study rooms."

Ten minutes later he returned, frowning.

"What's up?" April asked, wondering if something could have gone wrong already. It was unlikely, but knowing their luck, far from impossible.

"I'm all set for orientation tomorrow," he said. "But it goes until nine and it's downtown. That means that I won't be able to pick up Gram and bring her to the library."

April smiled faintly at Randall's use of her pet name for her grandmother. He, Thaddeus, and Dorian had all started to use it.

He was right. Randall had been picking up Gram and bringing her to the library every night for the past week so that they could go into the books that Gram found interesting.

"That's fine," April said. "We can skip a few nights."

"Maybe I could pick her up," Thaddeus said. "That's if you're okay with it, of course."

Randall didn't look convinced. "That's risky. What if you have an episode?"

Thaddeus shrugged. "I can't promise anything, but the number of episodes I've been having has decreased over the past couple of weeks—oddly enough, since we went into *The Strange Case of Dr. Jekyll and Mr. Hyde*—and those that I have had happened when I was at home, alone. Usually when I'm about to go to sleep." His expression soured, as though recalling an unpleasant memory.

"Hmm. He could drop me off at the downtown library and take the car," Randall mused. "What do you think, April?"

"I'm fine with it, as long as you're sure you're up to it, Thaddeus." Since they'd discovered that they could destroy all of the ink rot in a book simply by holding hands, she'd grown to trust Thaddeus. And he was right—he'd never had an episode in the library itself.

He nodded. "I am. Maybe we can pick Gram up before I drop Randall off, and she can drive the rest of the way, if it makes you feel better."

Who could argue with that logic? April nodded. "It's settled."

Chapter 2

That night Gram elected to visit the pages 0f *The Great Gatsby,* citing an affinity for the flapper style, to April's surprise.

Gram congratulated Randall on the job offer with a little good-natured teasing ("I think it's just wonderful that you're *actually* going to be working with April, Randall," Gram said as she and Randall entered the Werner Room. "Especially after so many months of *pretending* you do.")

When they readied to leave that night, Gram was still tapping her toes in time to the swing music. She was slightly tipsy. She'd allowed herself a single glass of champagne ("How can a girl refuse a drink from the hand of Jay Gatsby?") and the alcohol had gone straight to her head. She didn't seem to mind that she hadn't actually been able to dance.

"That was simply marvelous!" she said as the chair lift lowered her down the staircase. Thaddeus and Randall followed her progress, ever protective. April waited at the bottom.

Gram called down to her. "Can you believe he came and spoke with us? What a charming man, and so handsome!"

"Are you blushing, Gram?" April teased. She hadn't seen Gram so happy in a long time. Their trips into the books had restored some of the vitality she'd been missing while in the hospital. She hadn't even been this lively while planning their trip to Europe.

"Like a schoolgirl!" Gram crowed, then her smile tempered. "It's too bad how it ends for him. That little tart tears him to shreds, doesn't she?"

After climbing out of the lift, she looked up to the top of the stairwell where Dorian stood.

"You'll come over for dinner this weekend?" she asked him.

"I wouldn't miss it," he replied.

"Are you ready to go, Gram?" April asked.

Gram nodded, some of her fervor fading away. "Are you sure you have to stay late?"

April bit her lip. They hadn't told Gram about the ink rot, the black substance that slowly corrupted whole worlds if she—and now Thaddeus—didn't destroy it. Why make her worry, especially when she had so little time left? She was so happy now. "Like I told you, the gate requires a certain amount of maintenance. Boring stuff that I won't make you hang around for."

Gram sighed. "I suppose you're right. I'll get out of your hair. It is rather late for me—I haven't been up this late since I was in my fifties!"

They'd just gotten Gram into the passenger seat of the car and put her wheelchair in the trunk when April's phone rang. She pulled it out. "That's weird—it's the number for the Werner Room. Must be Dorian." She answered the call, then put the phone to her ear. "Hello?"

"Can you come up here? Bring Thaddeus and Randall. I need help with something," Dorian said. He sounded worried.

"We'll be right up." She hung up. "He asked if we can go upstairs. Gram, will you be okay out here for a few minutes?"

"Go on, all of you," Gram said, waving them away. "I'll wait here. I took a pain pill before we started down and I won't be much good to anyone, anyway. It's already kicking in."

"What is it?" April said once she, Thaddeus, and Randall were back upstairs. Dorian waited near the double doors. He held a book in his hands. It was covered in ink rot. It obscured so much of the cover that April couldn't tell if it had gone completely black.

April gasped, moving closer. "Did we miss one?" she said.

Dorian shook his head. "That's not possible. I checked the shelves after you left last night, just like always. This book wasn't like this then, I'm sure of it."

"Is there another outbreak?" Randall asked. "How does the rest of the collection look?"

Dorian shook his head. He looked terribly confused. "None of the other books have any rot on them at all, at least nothing that wasn't there before—and nothing this far gone."

"What book is it?" April asked.

Dorian hesitated before lifting the cover so that she could read the title page. *One Thousand and One Nights.*

April gasped. "Has it gone black?"

"We can read the title," Dorian said. "So no. But it's close."

"How long?"

"A few days. Maybe. Judging by the rate of growth, it could be much sooner."

She reached out and took the book. It didn't look like the ink rot she was familiar with. Rather than the usual moist, spore-like substance, this was dry, almost like the book had been charred over a fire.

April didn't like that it was different. New might mean something she wasn't able to fight.

April turned to Randall. "Can you take Gram home while Thaddeus and I take care of this? If she finds out about the rot..." she trailed off.

Randall nodded. "Of course."

April and Thaddeus had just turned toward the gate when April's phone vibrated in her pocket.

She pulled it out and looked at the screen. "It's Gram," she said to the others before hitting the accept button and pressing the phone to her ear. "Hey, Gram. What's up?"

"Hey, hon," Gram responded. The words were hard to understand, and languid, as though Gram were confused.

"Are you okay? You're slurring." The champagne had gone to her head, but she'd only had one glass. Surely it wasn't enough to actually make her drunk?

"I'm fine. Just the pain pill kicking in. Probably isn't mixing with the alcohol too well."

"Okay." April bit back a retort. Gram should have known better than to take a pain pill after drinking, especially with her low tolerance for alcohol. *She must really be in pain,* April thought, and her frustration softened. "What's up?"

"Your *friend* is here," Gram said, emphasizing the word *friend* in such a conspiratorial way that suggested April should know who she was referring to.

"Friend? What friend?" She looked around her. Dorian, Randall, and Thaddeus were all standing nearby. What other friends could she be talking about? Becky? Why would Becky be here in the middle of the night? "You'll have to be more specific."

She stepped over to the window and looked down at the parking lot. Randall had parked the car in the handicapped spot nearest the door.

A figure stood outside of the car window talking to Gram. The figure was tall, and not at all dressed appropriately for the weather in jeans, a hoodie, and old sneakers. The figure turned slightly, and even with the only light coming from the halogens in the parking lot, April recognized the rusty-red hair, the curve of the cheek, and the bulbous tip of his nose...

"You know, the one whose name you told me was Dorian?" Gram said into the phone. "The skinny red-head? Your supposed boyfriend? He wants me to bring him inside the library. He looks so cold, April. He doesn't even have a coat on. I told him you'd take care of him." Gram's voice became muffled. "Why don't you come sit inside the car while we wait for them to unlock the door?" Her voice became distant, like she'd pulled the phone away from her face. "These locks are such a pain. Drat. You know my fingers don't work the way they used to..."

"Gram, don't open the door," April said, panic rising in her throat. She wanted to believe that Barty had escaped the Collectors' clutches and was genuinely appealing to Gram on his own, but it was unlikely. Why would he talk to Gram first, rather than come to talk with them?

"Why not?" Gram said. "He's your friend, isn't he?"

April searched desperately for the words that would make Gram listen to her, but came up with only, "I'll be down in a minute, just *don't* let him in. I promise I'll explain."

Without hanging up the phone, April ran over to the loose floor board near the wall where the gate opened. She wrenched up the floor board. It was where the copy of *The Picture of Dorian Grey* that Dorian called home was kept open during the day so Dorian could cross over as soon as the gate opened at nine every night. The book wasn't the only thing that was kept there—they'd taken to hiding Silvis' pistol there when it wasn't in use.

She picked up the gun and rose to her feet without replacing the board. She hoped she wouldn't need it, but she knew better than to put faith in that hope.

"Care to tell us why you need that?" Dorian asked, his eyes on the firearm.

April almost dropped her phone in her haste to get downstairs. "Barty's outside with Gram," she called over her shoulder at the others.

"Barty?" Thaddeus said. "That's impossible. There's no way he could have escaped. The warehouse's security is too good."

"She's right," Randall said from the window overlooking the parking lot. "He's out there—alone."

"April, wait—" Dorian called after her, but she'd already made it down the staircase and was fumbling with the key to unlock the library door. The automatic door was off, or the door would have opened on its own...

Footsteps echoed down the staircase behind her. She had time to note that only Dorian was following her, but no time to wonder why Thaddeus and Randall weren't.

He'd made it halfway down the last landing by the time she'd turned the key in the lock and slid the door open. he was close on her heels as she ran out towards the figure standing just outside of Thaddeus' car.

She'd hoped it had been some mistake, that the man only resembled Barty enough to fool Gram. It wasn't a long shot, considering the pain meds coursing through Gram's bloodstream.

But seeing the mess of wild red hair—so much hair, especially since the Collectors had confiscated his bowler hat, which was magical and kept anyone who saw him from recognizing him, so of course they wouldn't let him keep it. Its absence was jarring.

"He didn't come here on his own. The Collectors must have sent him." Dorian warned over her shoulder. He was right—this was most likely a trap—but it was not one she could ignore, not when Gram was in danger.

"I know," she said and pointed the pistol at the back of Barty's head. She did her best to ignore Gram's cries, which shifted between frightened and confused that April had pulled a gun on someone. "I don't want to use this, Barty. Turn around and face me, slowly."

He did as he was told. At his side, he held a wand similar to the one up in her office. His other hand raised automatically in response to the pistol. He looked gaunt, as though he hadn't been eating enough. His skin had always been pale, but now it looked almost translucent. Being locked up underground for several weeks could do that.

His face always had a child-like quality. That hadn't changed, though now it was more feral, like a child left to fend for himself.

"Hey, Barty," she said.

"Hi, April," he said warily. "It's good to see you again." He nodded down at the wand. "I'm sorry about this. I don't have any choice."

"Just put it down, Barty," she said.

Randall and Thaddeus ran up behind her. Randall held the rifle and Thaddeus held the wand—he must have taken it from her office drawer, which was why he and Randall hadn't followed her down as quickly as Dorian had.

"Put the wand down," April repeated. "Then you can come inside. We'll help you."

"I can't, April," he said. "But you know that. My actions aren't my own." He lifted his free hand slowly towards his neck. Randall pumped the rifle and Barty winced. He paused, then carefully pulled his hoodie away from his neck, revealing a gray metal collar.

"Thaddeus can take it off," April pleaded.

"No, he can't."

"He's right," Thaddeus said. "I don't have the key. She does." He raised his wand and pointed it towards the evergreen hedges edging the parking lot.

A figure rose from behind the foliage. She was dressed all in black. Blond wisps of hair escaped from beneath a tight black beanie that hugged her skull. Silvis. She strolled toward them, her hips swaying with the terrible grace of a jaguar.

Thaddeus muttered a series of words. April still didn't understand their meaning, but she recognized it as the incantation he'd used to immobilize William the Bold when they'd gone into *The Strange Case of Dr. Jekyll and Mr. Hyde*.

Silvis froze in place. Unfortunately the spell didn't affect her ability to speak.

"Impressive, Broker," she said, her eyes locking with Thaddeus'. "Of course, I would expect no less from a former agent of your standing."

Randall turned his shotgun towards Silvis, whom he apparently viewed as more of a threat than Barty.

"Who is that, April?" Gram said from the car. She'd cranked the window open an inch. "Should I call the police?"

"Don't bother," Thaddeus said. "The Agency has influence over law enforcement. Even if your call goes through, no officers will be coming here tonight."

"It's okay, Gram," April said. "Just stay in the car and *do not* open the door. You're safe. I'll explain later."

Silvis smirked. "To be honest, I didn't think we'd get this far—we broke through one of your wards. Luckily good ol' Gram was here to invite Barty in. Can you imagine if she'd let us into the car, or even the main building?"

She was right; she shouldn't even have been able to get into the parking lot, but she'd managed to take two steps onto the black asphalt that marked the beginning of the library property. What if Gram hadn't called them? What if they'd been ambushed on their way outside?

"You were sloppy, Silvis," Thaddeus growled. "I trained you to do better."

"Yes, you did train me well." Silvis smirked. Her plan hadn't worked. Why didn't she seem more upset or concerned?

"I should kill you right here," Thaddeus growled.

"You should," Silvis said. "But you won't. I'd say the Pagewalker has made you soft, but that would give her too much credit. The truth is you've always been weak."

April looked at Thaddeus, concerned. His expression was dark, angry.

"Not in front of Gram," April hissed.

Thaddeus glanced at Gram. She'd rolled her window back up, and she now watched with one hand pressed over her mouth. Thaddeus' jaw hardened in anger, not at Gram, but at the fact that Silvis was right, at least about the fact that he wouldn't hurt her. He turned back to Silvis. "Where is the key to Barty's collar? You're too clever to have brought it with you."

"Of course I didn't bring it with me. And just so we're clear... Barty, tell them what will happen if something *unfortunate* should befall me."

Barty closed his eyes. "If you kill her, I'll kill myself as slowly and painfully as I can." The words came out stilted, as though Barty's lungs and mouth were going through the motions of forming them without cooperation from his brain. He was repeating, verbatim, a command that had been given to him.

Silvis' eyes narrowed. "And?"

"If you try to interfere with me or Agent Silvis, I'll kill myself as slowly and painfully as I can."

"They don't seem terribly concerned, scum," she said. "Demonstrate for them the extent of my control over you."

Barty's mouth pressed into a thin line. He pulled back the sleeve on his wandless arm. April gasped—the pale flesh was covered in long, thin scars. Some looked weeks old while others looked like they had only just scabbed over.

Barty lifted his wand and pointed it at the already-destroyed flesh. He muttered under his breath, and a fresh strip of skin began to peel away, as though lifted by an invisible pair of tweezers.

Barty winced, but continued to chant.

"Stop it!" April yelled. From the car Gram had turned her face away from Barty's self-mutilation.

"Release me," Silvis commanded, a smug expression appearing on her face.

Thaddeus held her gaze, his expression murderous. Barty's moans turned into high-pitched sounds that choked in his throat. Blood dripped down his arm and onto the snow.

"Do it, Thaddeus!" April yelled.

Thaddeus' lips pressed together in anger. He released his spell with an angry grimace. "Leave now," he said. "Next time, I *will* kill you."

Silvis smiled triumphantly. "That will do for now, scum. You can stop. Can't have you passing out on us again."

Relief filled April's chest as Barty's wand arm lowered. He carefully pulled the sleeve back down, hissing as it touched the unprotected wound. The faded fabric quickly grew dark with blood.

Hot tears pressed at the corners of April's eyes, but she refused to give Silvis the satisfaction of seeing them fall. "I'm sorry, Barty," she said.

"It's not your fault," he said, trying to smile through the pain. "It's not all bad. I'm learning magic from the other witches and wizards. I mean, it's only so The Collectors can use me later, but at least I get to learn. Ironic, right? It's what I always wanted."

"I'm going to get you out," April said. "I promise."

Barty smiled sadly. "Don't make promises you can't keep, April. There's too much—"

"That's enough talk, scum."

Barty's jaw clamped shut with a bony click, as though his top and bottom teeth had suddenly become magnetically drawn to one another.

"We're done here. Let's go."

With one last look back at them, Barty followed. April watched Barty's receding back, determined to watch them for as long as possible. They disappeared long before distance or the buildings should have offered them cover.

Gram started to open her door. "What the hell just happened?" she said. "Why was he doing that to himself?"

"Stay in the car, Gram," April said.

Gram looked like she wanted to protest, but did as she was told. The expression on her face told April that she'd be getting an earful later. April was fine with that. All that mattered now was that Gram was safe.

She turned to Thaddeus. "Why would she come here if she knew she wouldn't be able to get in?"

"She never meant to actually get in," Thaddeus said. "She's sending us a message."

"Are these normal tactics for Collectors?" April asked.

Thaddeus shook his head. "Silvis is different. Sadistic. And it seems that she's taken Mason's death personally."

"How were they able to get in the parking lot?" April asked. "I thought it was warded. What if we walked out to our cars and they ambushed us—"

"The parking lot *is* warded," Thaddeus sniffed. "The charm is time-sensitive—after nine—though anyone who's under the spell's protection can bring others in. Your grandmother is under the spell's protection."

"She must have invited Barty in." April kicked herself. Why hadn't she seen that Gram would be a weak link?

Thaddeus nodded. "After he was in, he would have been able to remove the ward on the parking lot itself, which gave Silvis access. Thank God she didn't invite him inside the building." He shook his head. "We should have been more careful."

Dorian spoke up. "This probably isn't the first time they've been here. They've most likely been watching, and tonight we just happened to leave Gram alone in the car, offering up an opportunity Silvis couldn't refuse."

April shivered at the thought of Silvis' eyes on her, on Gram, as they walked to their car every night. Poor Barty, out there without winter clothes on. She became even more thankful that Thaddeus and Randall were there to escort Gram home at night. "Did they break the ward on the car?"

Thaddeus walked around the car, considering it. He spoke a few words and pointed the wand. The car glowed subtly.

"Doesn't look like it." He flicked his wrist and the glow disappeared.

April nodded. "Good. Can you fix the ward on the parking lot? And maybe reinforce all of them?"

"I'll try," he said. He looked at Gram, who glared right back. "But you need to talk to her. Keeping her uninformed is a risk we can't afford. If she'd let Barty into the building..."

"I know," April said. "I will." It wasn't like she had much of a choice. Gram looked livid. There was no putting that cat back in the bag. "I'd better take her home. We'll discuss all this tomorrow."

She turned to get in the car, then turned back. "You should keep the wand on you. Just in case."

Thaddeus looked surprised. April had been keeping close tabs on the wand ever since what happened in *The Strange Case of Dr. Jekyll and Mr. Hyde*. Thaddeus had stolen the wand, planning to use it to overpower her. He'd changed his mind at the last moment and used it to save her instead. "Are you sure?"

"You're the only one who knows how to use it. I'll feel better if you have it. If you hadn't thought to grab it tonight..." she trailed off. Thaddeus thought that Silvis was just sending them a message, but if she'd seen any weakness in their defenses there was no doubt she would have taken advantage of it.

Thaddeus nodded. Were his eyes *misty?* "Thank you for trusting me," he said. "I don't deserve it."

April nodded. She'd placed her faith in Thaddeus several times before, and each time he'd betrayed it, up until he'd saved her. She hoped the new trend would continue, otherwise she'd have a lot of explaining to do to Dorian.

Speaking of explaining... Gram caught her eye. April sighed. They needed to get home.

After saying goodbye to the others, April got in the car and started driving. Gram said nothing. April tried to think of a way to break the tension, but everything sounded empty after what just happened.

When they got home, Gram walked up to the house without a word. She was tired and moved slowly, but April did not dare walk ahead of her, or even next to her. She trailed along behind, watching Gram's slow progress, the way she fumbled with her keys at the door.

"Gram," April said once they'd passed the foyer and the door was shut behind them, getting ready to explain.

Gram just held up a hand and shook her head as though April's voice caused her physical pain. "Are we safe here?"

April nodded.

"You're sure?"

April hated that Gram felt the need to ask. "Yes."

"Then not tonight. I need to sleep. And think."

With that, she walked down the hall and disappeared into her bedroom.

~~~

When April woke up the following morning Gram was already seated in the kitchen, waiting. A mug of green tea rested on the table in front of her, though no steam rose from the ceramic. April wondered how long she'd been there.

"Morning, Gram," April said cautiously. Gram threw her a cutting look, and April fell silent. She reached for the mug absentmindedly and took a long draw, grimacing, April guessed, at the tepid temperature. Gram liked her tea piping hot.

Gram placed the mug back on the table. "What happened last night?"

April had spent the night rehearsing what she'd say to Gram, but now words failed her. There was no easy explanation.

"It's complicated."

"I'm no rocket scientist, but I'm a smart enough woman," Gram said. "I can handle it."

"The gate is very... special," April said.

"No kidding."

"I mean rare. There are others who want it. An organization, sort of like the Illuminati or Freemasons, except real. We call them the Collectors."

"Collectors?" Gram pronounced the word as though it were in a hard-to-understand foreign language.

"Yes. They steal magic. They claim they're protecting the world. In reality they just want all the power for themselves."

"Those people last night—they were Collectors?"

April nodded, then shook her head. "The woman is. Her name is Silvis. Barty—the man you've met—he's our friend. They captured him about a month ago."

"Why did he hurt himself like that?" Gram asked.

"It was a show of power. He's a wizard—a magic user. The Collectors call them wielders. They keep the witches and wizards they capture prisoner so they can use their magic for whatever they want. He's wearing a collar that forces him to do whatever they say. Silvis wanted to scare us."

"Well, it worked on me." Gram said. April noticed the puffiness beneath her eyes. Had she slept at all the previous night? "That day in the mall, when that man tried to kidnap us—was he a Collector?"

"No. I mean, yes. He was. It was Thaddeus."

"*Thaddeus* is a Collector?" Gram's eyes widened. "Then why do you let him into the library?"

"He wasn't trying to kidnap us at the mall," April said. "He was saving us. There were Collectors in the food court. Silvis was there. She was coming to—" she stopped speaking. She'd been about to say *kidnap you,* but why make Gram any more upset than she already was? "She was coming after me. He saved us."

"So he *isn't* a Collector?"

"Not anymore. It's complicated, like I said." How was she supposed to tell Gram that Thaddeus had begrudgingly switched sides because he'd been driven crazy by the gate after literally eating it? Like that would go over well.

Gram's lips pressed into a thin line. "You need to get out of this. Call the library now and tell them that you quit. Promise me that you won't go back to that place."

"It's not that easy, Gram."

"It seems pretty easy to me."

"It's not. It's my job to keep the gate safe. Being able to step into the worlds is amazing, but that's only a small part of what this is. I can't abandon it, and I don't want to. Too many people are relying on me, Gram. Whole worlds. And I want you to keep coming so we can visit more worlds together. I don't want to lose that."

The corners of Gram's eyes glistened. "It's been amazing for me, too, dear. I've felt close to you again, closer than I've felt since you started working at the library." She paused. "Are you sure it's safe?"

April nodded. "We have protection—they're called wards—on the library and our houses, even our cars. The only reason they got into the parking lot is that Barty was able to appeal to you. I shouldn't have let that happen. I should have told you what was going on. I didn't want to burden you." She paused. "Will you come back tonight? Please?"

"Is there any way that I can talk you out of this?"

April thought for a moment. Was there? She answered honestly. "No."

Gram didn't speak for a long time. Finally she nodded, though reluctantly. "I'll come, but only to keep an eye on you. But you have to promise you won't lie again. And that you're safe. I don't care about this old bag of bones," she said, gesturing to herself. "I'm knocking on death's door, anyway. But you..." she trailed off. "Do you promise?"

April nodded. "I promise, Gram."

Gram returned the nod, but her face remained tight, worried as though she wasn't convinced. "I don't know, hon. I just don't know about this."

~~~

"Randall!" April said, surprised to see him and Rex sitting in their usual spot by the reference desk when she entered the Werner Room that afternoon. "Don't you have orientation in an hour? How long does it take to get there by bus?" City orientations were held in the downtown branch of the library, almost forty minutes away by car. She wasn't familiar with public transit—luckily—but she was pretty sure taking the bus took longer than driving.

"Longer than an hour," Thaddeus said. "He says he's not going. He thinks we need him here tonight, what with Silvis and Barty and the ink rot on that book. I don't entirely disagree with him."

Crap. April had all but forgotten the reason Dorian had called them back into the library in the first place. She hadn't even had time to process the fact that another book had started to go black, let alone that it was the genie's book.

She fought the urge to run to her office where Dorian would have put *One Thousand and One Nights* and check the book's condition. She stopped herself. No matter how bad it was, there was nothing she could do for it right now. She had to focus on getting Randall to the orientation.

"Whatever happens tonight, Randall, we can handle it."

Randall shook his head. "You need me. How can I go sit in some room downtown while you're in danger?"

"We'll be fine," April said. She wasn't sure if it was true, but she wasn't going to say that. She looked at Thaddeus. "Right?"

Thaddeus opened his mouth to speak, but April gave him a pointed look, one that she hoped transmitted the message that he needed to swallow whatever cynical remark he was about to make and convince Randall to go to the orientation.

Thaddeus faltered for a moment after he saw the look. When he finally spoke, he said, "It's unlikely that Silvis will show up again so soon. She might be unhinged, but she's also very calculative. She knows we'll have our guard up. She'll wait for a while, and if she shows up again it will be at a point when she can catch us by surprise."

"I would still feel better if I were here," Randall said. He crossed his arms over his chest. "I'll go to next month's orientation."

"You can't just not show up," April said. "You made a commitment. If you don't go today, you won't get another chance."

A library page pushed a cart through the Werner Room's double doors, and April got an idea. "No matter what you say, they've seen you here. They'll know you just didn't go. Becky and Janet put a lot of effort into getting you this job—do you want to disappoint them?"

Randall looked down. "They'd understand."

April nodded. "They would, if you could tell them the truth. But you can't. For the rest of the time you come to the library, you'll see them and know you let them down."

The library was Randall's refuge. April hated jeopardizing that sanctuary for him, even hypothetically. But she'd be damned if he was going to miss this opportunity.

"Do you really think they'd care that much?" The words were nonchalant, but the vulnerability beneath them was palpable. At his core, Randall didn't believe they would care.

"They cared enough to put on a big presentation about it at the last staff meeting. They collected endorsements from customers and staff. They really want this."

Randall looked down at his feet, where his service dog, Rex, lay. Rex must have been able to sense Randall's duress, because he rose and lay his head on Randall's knee with a tiny *humph* noise.

"See?" April said, pointing at the dog. "Even Rex thinks you should go."

Randall sighed and looked at Thaddeus. "You're sure that Silvis won't come back tonight?"

Thaddeus paused slightly too long before answering, and April raised her eyebrows and nodded in Randall's direction. Randall didn't see the look because his eyes were still on Rex.

"As sure as I can be, yes," Thaddeus said. "And even if she does, we have two guns, a magic wand, and an interdimensional portal. I think we can take her."

Randall pressed his lips together. Then he smiled, almost relieved. "It doesn't matter, anyway. I missed the bus. There's no way to get there on time."

"Sure, there is," April said. "Thaddeus can drive you. If you leave now you'll just make it."

~~~

Usually Gram would joke and chat as she rose up on the chair lift, but tonight she was silent, and it wasn't just because Randall was absent. The chair lift's motor seemed to whine louder than usual. That night Gram looked both ways as she entered the library, as though waiting for some attacker to jump out from behind one of the shelves.

Everyone was silent as they waited for Dorian to cross over. After he had, Gram cleared her throat.

"Be a dear, Dorian, and go stand with the others," she said. "There's something I need to say."

Dorian looked surprised—he wasn't used to taking orders—but he did as she told him to. He stood on April's left.

"I want to make one thing clear," Gram said, speaking in the same tone she used when April was in trouble as a kid. April might have laughed as the others stood at attention at the unusual harshness, but nothing about this situation was funny.

Gram looked at them over her glasses, not speaking until she'd made eye contact with each of them. Thaddeus and Dorian were both full-grown men, but each breathed in sharply when Gram's sharp gaze met theirs.

"I was shocked—and frankly disturbed—to find out that you all have been lying to me."

"We didn't lie—" April said, but before she could protest that it just hadn't come up, Gram turned her head slightly and gave her a hard look. April fell silent.

"A willful omission is the same as a lie," Gram rebuked her, and April couldn't argue. "I've been struggling with how to handle this. I had half a mind to never let April come back here."

April's heart chilled. If Gram wanted to keep April from the library, she'd undoubtedly find a way.

Gram continued. "After speaking with April this morning, I have decided—against my better judgment—to allow her to stay, but on one condition: No one will lie to me from now on. Do I make myself clear?"

"Yes, ma'am," the others mumbled, each looking down at his feet. Again, April felt the urge to laugh. She reminded herself that she was even deeper into Gram's bad graces than the others. That quickly killed the urge.

"Fine, then," Gram said. "I'll say the same to Randall when I see him next." She clapped her hands together. "Now, who's ready to visit the Alps?" the shift in tone from stern to bright was unnerving.

She walked over to one of the tables, and then Dorian approached her. He glanced furtively at Gram. "You and Thaddeus will have to take care of the ink rot in *One Thousand and One Nights* before you take your planned trip into *Heidi.*"

"Is it that bad?" April asked. "It can't even wait an hour?"

Dorian went and pulled the book off of the shelf. "I've never seen anything like it—the rot is moving so aggressively. Usually when that happens it affects the collection en masse, and the rapid growth slows after the initial onslaught. But to have it happen to only one book, and a book that you have a personal connection to at that, is strange."

"You think someone is doing this?" April asked.

"I don't see how," he said. "But you need to deal with it now—and proceed with more than the usual caution."

April nodded. "There's no need to worry. Thaddeus and I can erase any amount of rot with just a single touch, remember?"

"I know," Dorian said. He ran his fingers over the book's cover. "But I've never seen anything like this. This could be immune to your touch."

"What are you two whispering about over there?" Gram said, her eyes narrowing in their direction.

April sighed. "I'd better go explain it to her."

Dorian nodded. "Yes, you should. Not explaining things to her fully was an oversight. It almost cost us dearly."

April nodded. "I just didn't want to worry her, you know? I wanted her to think the gate was a beautiful, wonderful thing."

"It is," Dorian said.

"I know," she said. "But that's not all it is."

She walked to Gram. How was she going to frame this? She pulled out a chair and sat.

Gram raised an eyebrow at the motion. "What's going on?"

"You know the maintenance I do on the gate every night after you leave?"

Gram nodded.

April placed *One Thousand and One Nights* on the table between them.

Gram's eyes widened. "What a beautiful book," she said, then clucked her tongue mournfully. "How did it get burned like that? Was it in a fire?"

April shook her head. "It wasn't burned. It's called ink rot."

"Ink rot," Gram tried the words out, pausing between each one to see how it felt on her tongue. "Go on."

"No one's really sure. The library gate is complicated, Gram. I promise to tell you everything I know about it, but it's too much to do in one night. We don't have enough time. Basically, there's something wrong with the magic that connects the books to the gate. It degrades over time, and it shows up as ink rot. It consumes buildings, people, worlds... everything. I've seen it, and it's awful."

"Oh, sweetie, that sounds terrible. But what does that have to do with you?"

"It has everything to do with me. I'm the only one who can stop it," April said. "Every night I go in and erase ink rot."

"How?"

"By touching it," April said. She was about to tell Gram how dangerous the rot was for those who didn't have the power to erase it. But she didn't want to worry her. She'd never have to deal with that, anyway. "It's usually not this bad. We try to stay on top of it before it gets this extensive. I guess this book just slipped between the cracks."

Gram thought for a while, then she nodded. "Thank you for telling me. Is there anything else I should know?"

April shook her head. "No," she started to say, then corrected herself. "I mean, yes. But that's all I have time to say now. I'll explain everything later, I promise."

Gram nodded, considering her words. "I'll hold you to that promise. So no Alps tonight?"

April smiled. "I wouldn't bring you all the way out here for nothing. We're definitely going to the Alps. I just need to take care of this, first." She lifted *One Thousand and One Nights*.

Gram's brow furrowed in worry. "Is it dangerous?"

April breathed out, fighting the urge to say no. "It can be. But I've gotten very good at it. And I have my secret weapon—Thaddeus. As long as we work together, we should be done with this in no time. I'd say a half hour library time, tops."

"Library time?" Gram raised an eyebrow. "You mean how we can be in the book for so long and then we come back over here and almost no time has passed?"

April nodded. "Exactly."

"April?" Dorian called from the gate. "Are you ready?"

April nodded. She wheeled Gram over and parked her in front of the gate. "Dorian's going to stay with you," April said. "We like to leave at least one person on this side to make sure no one messes with the books while we're inside."

She'd been about to mention the Collectors but decided at the last minute not to. Why remind Gram of Silvis' visit if she didn't have to? It wasn't a lie. She needn't have bothered. From the dark look on Gram's face she was remembering just fine on her own.

"I'll be back soon," April said. "You decide what you want to do in the Alps, okay?"

Gram nodded, but she didn't look entirely convinced.

"Ready?" Dorian said. "Page sixty-three? Your usual door?" he said archly.

April nodded shortly, casting a quick glance at Gram. If she'd noticed Dorian mentioning the words "usual door" she didn't show it. Thank goodness. She had enough questions to answer as it was.

The gate began to widen. April had grown so used to the hissing sound that she barely noticed it anymore. Sandy dunes appeared on the other side, the landscape punctuated by the occasional tan-colored dwelling.

April looked over her shoulder at Gram. "I'll be back soon," she promised. To Thaddeus she said, "Let's go."

They stepped through the veil and April felt the heat wash over her face and limbs. After being in the chilly library it felt pleasant, like stepping into a sauna. She knew that soon the heat would grow uncomfortable and her body would be covered in sweat.

Thaddeus looked around, appraising the landscape. "So this is the desert, huh?"

April shrugged. "I guess."

He squinted. "Does anything seem *off* to you?"

April didn't know what he meant at first, but then her eyes widened. "Everything's so bright." Ink rot, especially in large quantities like the outside of the book indicated, had a light-sucking quality. Ink rot usually made everything seem muted, darker, like the air was filled with smog. The more ink rot, the darker and dingier the world seemed.

"Bingo."

"Isn't that a good thing?" April asked.

"I don't know. But we need to be careful. At the very least, we have to find the ink rot. I thought the benefit of having it spread so much was that it was easy to find."

"It usually is. Maybe it's concentrated in one spot?" April asked.

"I guess we'll know when we find it." He snapped his fingers. "Maybe your boyfriend can show us where it is. That genie guy."

April's face grew hot. "How do you know about him?"

"Randall mentioned it last night after we discovered the book. Also, from the way the genie showed up to save you, I knew there had to be something between you two."

He was referring to the time when the Collectors had infiltrated the library and the genie had used his magic to stop them—he'd literally forced them to walk backwards out of the library with a clap of his hands. That was before she and the genie had gotten romantically involved. Thaddeus had still been a Collector at that time, too.

April shivered at the memory. She hoped she'd never have to fight the genie. She was sure she'd lose.

"We weren't involved then," she said. "We'd just met. And he's not my boyfriend."

"I'm sorry. Do you prefer lover? Paramour? Booty-"

"Just stop," April said, glad when he fell silent. She didn't think she could keep her face from going crimson when Thaddeus said the words *booty call*. Then he would know.

"Fine," Thaddeus said, though he was still grinning. "But he might know where it is, right?"

"Maybe." April surveyed the sandy landscape, hoping she'd see the ink rot somewhere. She wasn't sure that she could deal with the genie at that moment.

"Where is he?"

"Usually he just appears," April said. "Or he teleports me to wherever he is. He always seems to know when I enter the world."

"Teleports you?" Thaddeus repeated, raising an eyebrow.

"Yeah. He can do that."

"Powerful guy. But I guess I knew that. Any idea why he hasn't shown up?"

"Nope."

"Think it has to do with the ink rot?"

April bit her lip. What if it did? What if the genie was in trouble? "I don't know. It's weird that he hasn't shown up yet. It could be because you're here."

"Do you know where he is?"

April nodded. She and the genie would sometimes walk back to the gate together, if the night was relatively cool. "I know the way."

She led him towards the town just off in the distance, and soon they were walking through the familiar cobblestone streets and tight sandstone alleys. Canopies spanned between most of the buildings, shading the street from the sun. Tan dust permeated every crack and coated every surface, and the sun streaked down, illuminating swirls of it kicked up by the feet of children and animals.

It was comforting to be back here. These hot streets were once her refuge. Were they still? She couldn't tell. Several times in the past week she'd thought about coming here, but something had stopped her. The genie didn't want a relationship, he'd made that abundantly clear. Being with him was self-destructive. Or was it?

She couldn't deny that she'd stopped coming here after Dorian had admitted his feelings for her. And she'd admitted—to herself, at least—that she also had feelings for him. But to get in a relationship with Dorian would be even more self-destructive than with the genie. Wouldn't it?

"Are you thinking what I'm thinking?" Thaddeus said, breaking her out of her thoughts.

"Probably not," she said. "What are you thinking?"

"That there's not a spot of ink rot in sight."

"You're right about that." The city was pristine. It didn't seem possible, considering how much had been on the book's cover. "We need to keep our guards up, at least until we know what's going on. Do you have the wand on you?"

He nodded, his hand patting the inside pocket of his coat.

"Good. Keep it at the ready." She nodded toward the building up ahead. "That's it. The House of Fire."

Several women stood out front dressed in fine silks, beckoning to the passing men and even some of the women. Playful but alluring, promising the experience of a lifetime—or at least a night of fun.

"The one with all the prostitutes in front of it?" Thaddeus said.

"They prefer the term courtesan, and yes. The genie owns a brothel. Randall didn't mention that?"

"He certainly didn't," Thaddeus said with a raised eyebrow.

"Is it a problem?"

Thaddeus shrugged. "No."

"Good."

April pushed past the women, Thaddeus following close behind her.

She stepped inside. The genie's chair—more of a throne, really—was empty. A couple women tittered as they entered, whispering behind their hands.

Asima, a slim woman with light brown eyes and wavy brown hair that she kept swept up above her head, sat at a small table nearest the genie's throne, pushing beads around on an abacus. One of the oldest women at the House of Fire, Asima had slowly risen to the top, her role becoming mostly managerial—someone had to keep the genie in line. If he was the owner, Asima would be the general manager—or madam, as she referred to herself. Asima was one of the few faces that April had seen almost every time she'd come to see the genie.

Today it was no different, right down to the look of annoyance as her eyes fell on April.

April walked over to Asima. "Where is he?"

Asima did not even glance up from the abacus. April respected Asima's ability to rise to a secure position of relative power, but Asima had never liked April much. "In his chambers—where else? I'd show you but you know the way."

April nodded, not letting Asima's chilliness fluster her. She started to down the passageway that led to the genie's suite, but the Asima side-stepped her, placing a hand on the stone between her and Thaddeus, blocking his way before he could even take a step.

"What's your pleasure, love?" she asked, pressing her sizeable bosom out so that it almost touched Thaddeus. "I can be that and more."

Thaddeus smiled wryly. "For most men, I'm sure you could. But not for me."

"Someone younger, perhaps?" If she was hurt by the perceived rejection, she hid it well, though April thought she caught a slight downturn of her lips. She waved at the throng lounging on the pillows, never taking her eyes away from Thaddeus.

The courtesans began to rise, but Thaddeus motioned for them to stay put. "That won't be necessary. Even if I had the time, no woman is to my liking."

Asima's mouth opened in surprise, but she quickly recovered. She bowed her head and stepped away. "My apologies. I'm usually better at reading a customer's needs. I can send for one of our young men? I'm afraid the selection is smaller, but I'm sure we can find someone who will tickle your fancy."

Thaddeus cleared his throat. "No need. I'm here on business." He nodded towards April.

"Oh," Asima said flatly, her professional air falling away, suddenly becoming disinterested. "You're with her. My mistake. I didn't realize she had friends." She went and sat back down behind the desk, returning her attention to the abacus.

Thaddeus cleared his throat and nodded to April, who realized that her mouth had fallen open.

"Sorry," she said. "I mean, I didn't know that you're gay."

Thaddeus shrugged. "It doesn't come up much in conversation—especially with my enemies. Does it change anything?"

"Of course not."

"Then it doesn't matter. I've never had time for relationships, anyway."

April nodded. That was that. She led Thaddeus back to the genie's chamber. When they entered he was lying on his bed, asleep.

She'd never seen the genie asleep before. If she'd been asked, she would have said that he didn't sleep. But here he was, his mouth slightly open, eyes closed.

"Genie?" she said, and his eyes opened faster than she would have expected of someone who'd just woken up—and he didn't look tired or groggy at all. Damn magical beings, waking up looking perfect with no effort.

"Sorceress," he said. "You're here." He glanced at Thaddeus. "And you brought a visitor. At least it's not that pretty-boy."

April raised an eyebrow. "Dorian is back in the library. This is Thaddeus."

The genie glanced over at Thaddeus. His eyes narrowed momentarily before his face broke out into a grin.

"You're the one who invaded the Sorceress' room of books." He turned back to April. "I saved you from him, remember?"

April nodded. "You did."

The genie held her gaze for a moment longer, then he turned back to Thaddeus. "And now here you are, accompanying her on her journeys. It's amazing how you can be in someone's bad graces one moment, and good graces the next. Or vice versa. My, how things change." He turned back towards April when he said the last few sentences, his tone serious, almost angry.

He rose, revealing that he wasn't wearing a shirt, showing off his muscular chest and shoulders. Luckily he wore a pair of the loose silk pants he favored. They were always brightly patterned, reminiscent of the designs on an Indian sari. This one was a yellow and pink paisley pattern. He reached for a silk tunic with a corresponding pattern.

When he spoke again, his tone was neutral. "So what brings you here? I assume it's not the usual, since you've brought a friend with you."

April chose not to answer his question right away. "Why didn't you come to get me?"

"Am I your keeper?" the genie said. "I didn't know you were here."

"But you always know that I'm here. You didn't know this time because you were asleep?"

There was a flash of confusion, possibly fear on the genie's face, but it disappeared so fast that April was sure that she had misread his expression. "Precisely."

"Since when do you need to sleep?" April asked, crossing her arms. "I've never seen you sleep before. Aren't you the one who always said things like 'beds aren't for sleeping?'"

Thaddeus snorted behind her, but she was too worked up to care.

"I don't need sleep," the genie said archly. "But there hasn't been much to do. I was bored." His gaze softened, and he stepped towards her. "This is not how I pictured our first reunion going, especially after you've been gone for so long."

He leaned in and pressed his mouth to hers. She felt the same fire spark between them as always, but something about it felt wrong. She put her hand on his chest, which was so hot that it nearly burned her palm. She cleared her throat and nodded toward Thaddeus, who didn't look as embarrassed as he did annoyed.

"Should I arrange for a distraction for your friend? I can have Asima call for someone?"

"No, thank you," Thaddeus said curtly. "She already offered. We're here on business."

"Business?" the genie said, looking down at April.

She nodded. "We found evidence that there's extensive ink rot here. It popped up overnight and completely took us off guard. The case is bad enough that it puts your world in jeopardy. But we're here and we see no sign of it." She paused. "Do you know what I'm talking about? Have you seen anything like that?"

The genie sighed. He would know what ink rot looked like, since April had talked about it to him at length.

"Come. It's in the marketplace."

"So you do know where it is," April said. "Why didn't you say so right away?"

The genie's expression grew pinched. "I knew what it was the moment I saw it. It didn't seem terribly advanced, and I assumed you would show up sooner or later to combat it. I figured we would have a reunion first. I didn't realize the situation was so dire."

He stepped forward without looking at her, his demeanor that of a sullen child who hasn't gotten their way.

Thaddeus walked up to stand beside her. "Seems like someone's upset."

"He's just pouting," April said.

"I don't mean to pry, but why *did* you stop coming here to see him? Did you two have some sort of lovers' spat?"

"He's not—"

"Your lover. I know. Don't dodge the question."

April sighed. "Nothing happened between us. I... I guess I don't know why." She paused, not wanting to tell him it was because she was confused by her feelings for Dorian, if that was what they were. She hadn't even fully processed this herself. "Let's get this over with."

They started towards the marketplace, at least a twenty-minute walk from the brothel. The genie walked several paces ahead of them without speaking, which wasn't like him. He was always bragging about one thing or another, or pointing things out in the surrounding streets, as though he were personally responsible for each of the city's wonders.

They walked in silence until they had to stop at an intersection. April went up and stood next to the genie, unable to see what had caused the clot of people in front of her.

"What's the hold-up?"

"A herd of goats is crossing. We'll be here a while." He crossed his arms and fell back into silence.

April looked around and saw that Thaddeus had stepped away from them, giving them room to speak. The gesture seemed obvious, and he seemed bent on pretending he couldn't see them.

April spoke. "Did I do something to piss you off?"

The genie still didn't look at her. "What you do is no concern of mine."

"Well, you're not acting like it. You've been weird ever since I refused to let you command one of your underlings to seduce Thaddeus."

"Can you blame me for expecting something more special for our first reunion after you've neglected me for so long?"

April rolled her eyes. "You're talking like we're in a relationship. You were the one who was always going on about how that's *not* what this is."

He opened his mouth to speak, but then shook his head. "Never mind. It doesn't matter." He nodded in front of them. All the goats were gone, and the crowd was dispersing. "The road's clear. Let's go."

He stepped forward without looking at her. Had she hurt his feelings?

Not knowing what else to say, she followed two paces behind him, silent. Thaddeus fell into step beside her.

"Everything all right?" he said.

"Not even a little. Why are men so stupid?"

Thaddeus shrugged. "That bad, huh? Want to talk about it?"

She shook her head. "No. Let's just get this over with so we can get out of here."

Her heart twisted. It wasn't that easy. The genie was hurt, and even though she hadn't seen it coming, she couldn't just leave him to suffer. He'd comforted her during some of the hardest times of her life. He'd always been kind to her, and seemed to be kind to others, too—when he wasn't having a tantrum or trying to show off. Had she misjudged him? Maybe he was more sensitive than she'd thought.

They entered the market. Thaddeus observed its comings and goings with interest. April realized that she'd grown used to the marketplace, but remembered how fantastical it had seemed the first few times she's walked through it, like being in a movie.

She looked around with renewed appreciation. Nearby, two men argued over a goat tied to a stake between them. The goat chewed on grass complacently, unaware of its impending fate as a meal. The men continued to bicker over the price until one man, the buyer, waved his hands dismissively and started to walk away. The seller waited ten seconds before calling after the man. He made an angry show of being taken advantage of as the other man paid him and led the goat away.

April smiled. Gram had once told her that a bargain wasn't good unless both parties felt cheated. Of course, she'd been talking about yard sales, not goats.

They walked past a stall selling a hot beverage that might have been coffee or tea or neither out of a large bubbling kettle. Men crowded around the man sweating over the boiling liquid as boys selling biscuits and food weaved between them.

The genie stopped, pointing to a corner between two buildings. Hardly anyone walked there.

"There's your ink rot," the genie said. "Now take care of it and go. I trust you know how to get back to your door on your own."

He turned on his heel to leave, but April called back at him.

"Stay," she said.

He almost didn't turn, but did after a few moments, reminding her of the seller who'd started to walk away. "Why?"

"Because I might need you," she said. She realized as they left her mouth that the words could be taken in more than one way.

The genie thought for a moment, then nodded. "Fine."

They walked to the corner, Thaddeus speeding up to fall into step beside April. As they approached, small spots of darkness that April had taken for shadows cast by the buildings and canopies became darker, more prominent. It didn't look like any ink rot she'd seen before; it resembled fire damage more than spore-like rot. The very center followed the familiar spiral pattern, but around it everything was charred and haphazard, with bits of blackened material flaking away. It looked almost like there had been a fire. Even the part that looked familiar was covered in a thin, ash-like material.

"Have you seen anything like this before?" Thaddeus asked.

April shook her head. "No. The shape at the center is familiar, but that's it."

"Do you think we can combat it?" Thaddeus asked.

"Only one way to find out." She stepped towards the rot, holding her hand out to Thaddeus. He took it.

The genie took a step forward as well, unable to fully maintain his façade of indifference. He watched them intently.

April held fast to Thaddeus' hand, and reached out and gingerly touched the edge of the scorched rot. Nothing happened.

"What's wrong?" Thaddeus asked.

"I don't know," April said. "It's not working. But the rot also isn't fighting back." Normally the rot would start to attach itself to anyone foolish enough to touch it, slowly absorbing and feeding on their life force.

"Is it *dead*?" Thaddeus asked.

"I don't think so," April said. "I'm not even sure that the rot can die, you know?"

Thaddeus nodded. He did know. Having been attached to the gate, he had the same innate sense about gate-related things that she did. His wasn't as sharp, though.

The genie stepped forward. "What's happening?"

"The rot should have gone away when we touched it," April explained. "It didn't work. It doesn't seem to be spreading, though. You said it's been here for a while?"

"Yes, almost two weeks." The genie bit his lip.

Thaddeus narrowed his eyes, considering the rot. "You're the Pagewalker. What do you want to do?"

April thought for a second. "I think Dorian will want to get a good look at this. He might have seen something like it before."

"Do you really need to talk to him?" the genie said. He looked suddenly nervous. Did he really dislike Dorian that much?

"He has more experience with ink rot than anyone. If he hasn't seen this before, then we know it's something new."

"You said yourself that it doesn't seem to be spreading or causing any harm. Can't you just go back to your world? Maybe it will go away on its own."

April shook her head. "That's not how ink rot works. If you don't kill it at the source, it spreads and spreads until it takes over the world." Even the genie, who cared about no one but himself, shouldn't want that to happen.

The genie fell silent. "I didn't know that," he said.

"I've told you that before."

"I must have misunderstood. Go to your pretty boy, then."

April was fine with letting the genie get back to wherever he was going, but Thaddeus spoke. "You should come with us. Dorian might have some questions for you."

"Why would I do that? He's the last person I want to see."

"Look," Thaddeus said, "Historically I'm no fan of his, either, but it's what's best for your world, and therefore it's what's best for you. What if you know something that Dorian will recognize?"

"I've given you my answer," the genie said, lifting his chin.

Anger flared in April's chest. Gram was back at the library waiting for them, and the genie was acting like a petulant child. "What's the big deal?" she said.

"It seems to me that he's afraid to talk to Dorian," Thaddeus said airily. April couldn't tell if he knew that this would push the genie's buttons, or if he'd just gotten lucky. It was hard to tell with Thaddeus, but she'd put her money on the former.

"I am not afraid," the genie said through gritted teeth. His eyes flamed, and for a moment April thought he was going to unleash his fiery magic on Thaddeus, but he only turned his back on him.

"Damn you and the limitations you've placed on me, sorceress," he said. "I think I would have preferred to be under the control of that stupid magician. At least with him I had a chance of escaping intact. Now I am little more than a castrated beast of burden."

He was talking about the condition that April had put on his freedom when she'd given him his ring back: He couldn't harm anyone using magic. She'd known that he resented the terms, but he seemed to have done well enough for himself.

"Do you really need to *hurt* people to feel"—she struggled to find the right word—"*Manly*? That's pathetic."

"Isn't it? I cannot defend myself, or my honor. No one knows, but if they were to find out..." He turned towards her, his eyes flashing again. "In spite of that, I am not afraid of that golden-haired pretty boy!"

Thaddeus held up his hands. "I'm just calling it like I see it."

The genie turned back towards her, his expression murderous. "Fine," he said. "Let's go see if *Dorian* call solve this problem."

He led them back through the city streets. They walked for ten minutes in total silence, thankfully. If this was how the genie was going to act, she was glad she hadn't come to see him for so long.

It seemed to take forever to reach the gate. April wished they'd let the genie go on his way. His presence was like a storm cloud looming over their heads, making the air heavy.

Once they'd finally arrived back at the gate, April stepped through the veil. Gram sat in one of the chairs next to Dorian.

"Back so soon?" she asked, raising an eyebrow at April. "Dorian was just telling me more about these ink-rotted books."

Thaddeus stepped through behind her, followed by the genie.

Dorian's expression soured when his eyes fell on the genie. Whatever bad blood the genie had with him, it was mutual. "I guess things didn't go as smoothly as we hoped."

The genie ignored Dorian, his eyes sparkling as they fell on Gram. "And who are you?" he said. "I don't believe I've had the pleasure."

April was confused by the genie's change in tone. It was suddenly soft, almost simpering. Surely he knew this was Gram; she'd talked about her before.

"I'm April's Grandmother," Gram said, her eyes narrowing.

"No," the genie said. "You must be her mother, or maybe an aunt. You're far too young to be her grandmother."

Gram blushed. April couldn't tell if she was buying into the genie's flattery, or if she was just embarrassed by the attention.

'Stop it, you," Gram said. "And you are?"

"A friend of April's."

Gram opened her mouth as if to speak, but her body was wracked with a coughing fit. She held her handkerchief to her mouth, and red-streaked phlegm marred it when she pulled it away.

The genie looked down at the stained handkerchief, his brow furrowed. "You're not well. Do you mind if I help you?"

He held up his hands as though to touch her, but waited for her permission. Gram glanced at April nervously. Maybe she didn't want to be rude, because she turned back to him and nodded.

He placed on hand on her upper back and one hand across her chest, just below her collar bone. Gram looked uncomfortable at first. "You're hands are very warm," she said, then her eyes widened. "Almost hot..."

She yelped, pulling away from the genie. As she opened her mouth a warm red glow emanated from the back of her throat, and a small amount of steam billowed out.

She rose and backed away from the genie. "Well, I never! How—"

She stopped mid-sentence, her hand touching her chest. Her voice was strong and clear. She hadn't even noticed how weak it had gotten.

"I feel amazing," she said. "What did you do?"

"The effects will wear off soon, I'm afraid," the genie said. "Even I cannot stop the hand of time. But I thought you might welcome a reprieve."

Gram looked conflicted. Finally she said, "Thank you. It's... nice to breathe normally again, even if it's only for a little while."

The genie inclined his head, a surprisingly gracious gesture.

"I'm glad you feel better," Dorian said to Gram. His words sounded sincere, but it was obvious that he wished what made Gram feel better was something other than the genie's magic. He turned to April and Thaddeus. "What happened? Why is *he* here?"

The genie crossed his arms, his upper lip pulling back in a sneer. "I'm not thrilled to see you, either. April wanted me to come."

April winced, then told him about the strange rot. She finished with, "We thought he might be able to describe things for you better than we could. He might know something we don't."

Dorian's creamy white skin became ruddy and splotched with red around his cheeks. "Describe it, then."

"Gladly, if it quickens my departure from this place. There's a corner of your 'ink rot' in the marketplace. It's been there for weeks without change. Most of the city dwellers don't seem to notice it—I suppose that's because they don't have access to magic. A few days ago it started to change, grow bigger. Then they showed up." He nodded to April and Thaddeus.

"Is that it?" Dorian asked.

"Yep."

"Not very helpful," Dorian said, matching the genie's snide tone. Dorian rarely allowed himself to speak in such a way—he would refer to it as "common."

The genie held up his hands. "I never said I knew anything. It wasn't my idea to come here."

"That's not all," Thaddeus said. "This ink rot is different than anything I or even April have seen before. It looks more like burn marks, or maybe smoke damage."

"You left that part out," Dorian said to the genie.

"If *they* can't tell the difference, why would I be able to?" the genie said through clenched teeth.

They started to squabble, and Gram walked over to April. She'd been watching the genie with interest ever since he touched her. April had tried to ignore the pointed looks Gram kept throwing at her.

"Can I talk to you a minute, hon?" she whispered. "In private?"

"Sure," April said. Dorian and the Genie were too busy arguing to notice her absence.

Gram led her into the stacks, her grip on April's wrist firm and strong. Tears pricked the corners of April's eyes. She wished more than anything that what the genie had done was permanent, that Gram could be this healthy forever.

"What's up, Gram?" she said when they had a shelf between them and the others. She hoped Gram didn't notice the extra wetness in her eyes. "Are you not feeling well? Do you want to go back to the house?"

If she was being honest, it was probably best if Gram went home. There was no telling how long it would take to figure out what was going on with the rot, if they even managed to figure it out tonight. At least it didn't seem to be spreading, as the genie had pointed out.

"No, it's not that," Gram said. "I feel better than I've felt in months—that man's touch really packs a punch. It's just... how many of these men have you been intimate with, hon?"

April's mouth fell open. "What? Gram, no. What would give you that idea?"

"There's no reason to be embarrassed. I just want to make sure you're making good decisions... *and* being safe."

"First of all, this is a really uncomfortable conversation to be having with my grandmother—no offense. Second, what would give you the impression that I've slept with *any* of them?"

"Well, they're obviously fighting over you. And don't forget that you told me your boyfriend was Middle Eastern, which that man very clearly is, and also that his name was Dorian, which, obviously, is Dorian's name. Then you brought that boy who showed up last night to the house—"

"Barty," April said, and then because she felt like the least she could do was call him by the name he preferred, she corrected herself. "Bartholomew, actually."

Gram nodded this new information away. "Right, Barty. So that's *three men*." She looked at April pointedly. "Am I wrong? I assume you haven't slept with Thaddeus, since he's gay."

"How do you know that? I only just found out." April shook her head. "You know what? Never mind. And you're wrong."

"Oh? So you haven't slept with any of them?"

April was about to say yes, but then she faltered. "I mean, not *all* of them. Not even most of them." She sighed. "Only with the genie."

"Genie, huh? I suppose that explains the magical healing touch." Gram looked skeptical. "So why did you tell me that his name was Dorian?"

"When you asked, I panicked and wasn't able to come up with a good name on the fly. The only one that popped into my head was Dorian. Trust me—I wish that I'd picked any other name on the planet." She paused. "I also thought that if I told you I did have a boyfriend that it would make you worry less about me being home late."

"Why not just tell me his real name?" Gram asked.

April flinched. "Because I don't know it. Was I just supposed to say his name is 'genie?'" She thought about this for a moment. "Actually, that might have turned out better in the long run."

"You slept with a man whose name you don't know? More than once?" Gram raised an eyebrow. "I did some risqué things in my youth, but that takes the cake."

"Djinn are very protective of their names. It never seemed to matter much."

If April was being honest, she'd never wanted to know the genie's name. Not knowing made everything seem more intense, more destructive. And that's what she wanted at the time. Was it what she still wanted?

The argument happening in front of the gate grew louder. April peered through the books to make sure they weren't going to kill each other—the genie couldn't use magic to hurt others, but he could certainly use his fists. Dorian was shaking his finger at the genie. Annoying, yes, but hardly threatening.

"Dorian likes you, you know," Gram said. "A lot."

"How do you know?" April asked.

"By the way he looks at you and talks about you. By the care he takes when he's around you. How do you feel about him?"

April sighed. "It doesn't matter. It wouldn't work out. We've talked about it before."

That wasn't quite true, was it? Dorian had done the talking. April had never gotten to say how she felt. She was glad for it at the time, because it meant she didn't have to parse out her own complicated emotions, but what would Dorian say if she told him? Would it change anything?

They were silent for several seconds, listening to the bickering. Finally Gram spoke. "For what it's worth, I don't think it's a coincidence that you told me his name before."

April nodded. It still didn't change anything. "Let's go back out there before they kill each other."

When they moved back around the shelf, Dorian and the genie were posturing at each other.

"Are you guys done?" April said. "None of this is helping us figure out what's going on with the ink rot." She turned to Dorian. "So ink rot with scorch marks shows up heavily on the outsides of books but not really on the inside—have you seen it before?"

Dorian held the genie's eye contact for several seconds before turning to look at April. "Never. I've never seen anything like that. But I'll need to take a look to be absolutely sure." He bit his lip. "If it has changed, I wonder what caused it."

"In my estimation, it could be one of two things," April said. "Either it was caused by Thaddeus eating the threshold—"

"Eating *what?*" Gram said.

April patted Gram's elbow. "I'll explain later. It was either that, or—"

"—Jekyll's potion," Thaddeus finished with her. So he'd felt it, too.

"Jekyll's potion?" Dorian said, his brow furrowing. "You mean how it created the ink rot monster? That was in a completely different book."

April struggled to find the words to explain. "The ink rot exists beyond the books, right? It's all connected. Thaddeus and I can eradicate all the ink rot in an entire book with one touch, but the rot in other books isn't affected. But it's also still all connected, somehow."

"You're saying it's all one thing? The ink rot?"

April blinked. "Well, yes. Didn't you know that?" she'd thought this fact was obvious, even when she'd first started her role as Pagewalker.

Dorian shook his head. "No, I didn't."

"I feel it, too," Thaddeus said. "It's like a fungus, or a hive. A million different parts, each distinct, but part of a greater whole."

"And you think Dr. Jekyll's serum affected *all* of the ink rot? In every world?" Dorian ran his fingers through the blond curls that haloed his face.

A terrifying thought occurred to April. "What if I can't fight it? What if it's developed some kind of immunity to my touch?"

"I don't think so," Dorian said, too quickly. "I mean, you and Thaddeus defeated the ink monster."

"True," she said, "But I couldn't fight it on my own. I needed Thaddeus' help." April grimaced at the memory of the ink monster. What if another monster showed up in every book? She and Thaddeus could fight them, of course, but it raised the stakes. And it showed that the ink rot could evolve, adapt. She wasn't sure that was something her magical ability to destroy the rot could do.

What if the ink rot adapted beyond that, so that even together they couldn't fight it? Was that what was happening now?

She hoped Dorian would reassure her, but he avoided her gaze. "Let's go," he said.

They turned towards the gate, but the genie seemed to think they were looking at him. "What are you looking at me for?" he said. "I don't know anything about this." He crossed his arms.

April sighed. "No one's waiting for you to give us any answers. We just need to go back in, okay? Geesh."

The genie's eyes widened. "Oh."

April turned to Thaddeus. "Can you stay and watch the books?" She raised her eyebrows to add the unspoken clause, *and Gram?*

It made her uneasy to leave Thaddeus behind. It meant she'd have to deal with the ink rot on her own. But leaving Gram alone was not an option. She wished Randall were there, though she wouldn't have pulled him from orientation for anything.

Thaddeus nodded. "Since our little hand-holding trick doesn't work, I'm of no use, anyway." He turned to Gram. "Looks like it's just you and me."

"Great," April said. "Let's go." She turned to the genie, who was already preparing to step over the gate's threshold. "Are you going to come with us to the market, or are you heading back to the House of Fire?"

She'd hoped he'd choose the latter. Instead, he said, "I'll come with you. If only to prove that I'm no coward."

She sighed. Now she'd not only have to deal with his sullenness, she'd have to listen to him and Dorian bickering. Great.

Before joining April and Dorian in front of the veil, the genie took Gram's hand. "It's been a pleasure to meet the woman who raised April. If you're ever in my city, you need only to ask for me at the House of Fire."

Gram blushed again as the genie bowed to her, and then he stood next to them. They stepped through the gate, and for the third time that day the genie led them to the corner of the marketplace where the ink rot was located.

They walked halfway there in silence, her and Dorian standing shoulder to shoulder and the genie stalking ahead of him, his fists clenched at his sides. The crowd parted wherever he went. April wasn't sure if it was because his reputation preceded him or if the crowd could sense how angry he was. She wondered if they knew he was a djinni. Except for the few brief moments where his eyes would flash flames, he looked human to her.

They passed a stall selling kabobs. "Want some?" Dorian said. He seemed to be trying to lighten the mood.

"Right now?" she said. They had work to do.

"If it's as stable as you say, the ink rot can wait," he said. "I thought it would break up the tension. Sorry that I allowed him to bait me."

April raised an eyebrow. "You did your fair share of baiting, yourself."

His expression became sheepish. "I suppose I did. Let's just keep going. You're right. We don't have time for distraction."

He started to walk forward, but April reached out and grabbed his hand to stop him without even thinking about it. He glanced down at her hand, and she dropped it.

"A kabob sounds good. We need to eat, anyway." She paused. "If I'm not mistaken, that's the cart we ate at the first time we came into this book."

Dorian's face broke out into a grin. "You remembered," he said. "I'll be right back."

April watched him walk away, feeling suddenly carefree in spite of all that was happening.

"Does he think he can buy your affection with hunks of skewered meat?"

She turned to see the genie standing behind her, his arms crossed. He watched Dorian walk towards the cart.

"He's not trying to buy my affection," April said defensively. "We're friends. He's just a genuinely nice person. I suppose you wouldn't know what that looks like."

The genie scoffed. "Don't be fooled. Men are only nice when they want something."

"You're not even nice when you want something."

April winced as the words left her mouth, not anticipating the genie's hurt expression. The words weren't fair—the genie could be generous, and she'd never seen him be cruel to the people who worked for him—and hadn't he just given Gram a wonderful gift? The hurt disappeared behind his normal callous façade almost immediately, but not soon enough to keep her from seeing it.

"Was I not good to you?" he said. "Am I not a fair employer? I don't understand why you think I'm a monster."

He sounded so... *vulnerable.* Had April ever seen him allow even a tiny glimpse of weakness to show? She didn't think so.

"You're right. That wasn't fair. You've just been acting like a jerk since I got here."

She turned to check on Dorian, nervous that he might reappear and overhear their conversation. But what did it matter? They were only friends, despite what Gram said, and he knew about her relationship with the genie, even encouraged it.

"Don't worry," the genie said. "It will take the cook a good five minutes to get your food ready. A lazy man, that one."

"He encouraged me to see you, you know." April didn't know why she wanted the genie to know this.

"The cook?"

Her lip curled. "You know exactly who I'm talking about. Dorian."

The genie's expression became serious. "That, more than anything else, betrays how strong his feelings are for you. He wants to put as many barriers as possible between the two of you, so that he doesn't have to be the one to choose, to make a decision." He paused. "What I never anticipated are your feelings for him."

"What feelings?" April looked away.

"You don't have to lie to me. It's in the way you look at him, the way you say his name. Would you say my name that way?"

"I don't even *know* your name," April said. It was too much, especially since Gram had said almost the exact same thing to her only minutes before.

"You're avoiding the truth," the genie said. They lapsed into a minute-long silence. April figured their conversation was over, but then the genie said, "And you're wrong, by the way." His voice sounded flat, tired. It reminded her of a balloon that had been so filled with hot air that it burst. Defeated.

"About what?"

"I do care about others beside myself." As though worried she might protest and shoot him down, he rushed to get his next words out. "I care about those under my employ, Asima and the girls. I care about you. It hurt me more than I expected when you stopped coming to see me."

April's eyes widened. "You're the one who always made it clear that this thing between us was just fun."

"You're right. I never anticipated that *you* would shun *me*."

"Oh, so you're allowed to be free, but I have to be bound to you? That's really messed up."

The genie pinched the bridge of his nose. It was an incredibly human gesture. "No, that's not what I meant. I—"

"You were just so full of yourself that you thought I wouldn't be able to resist coming to see you."

"Yes. Sort of, but that's not the whole picture. I never presumed to own you or solely command your affections, but I never thought you'd stop coming to see me. When you did, I was caught off guard by how much it affected me. I spent days awaiting your arrival, but then you stopped showing up at all."

All of this was coming so fast. "What are you trying to say?"

He took her hands, stooping down so that he was looking directly into her eyes. His were completely human, a brown so dark that they were almost black. "I don't want to lose you. I am willing to give up my freedom if it means that you keep coming to see me."

"Are you saying you want... to be in a relationship?"

"If that's what it takes, yes. If that's what *you* want. The concept is foreign to me, but I'm willing to do anything if it means I get to keep seeing you."

April felt overwhelmed, unable to think. She'd been avoiding the genie for a reason, that was true. What was the reason? Was it because she liked him but knew that visiting him was self-destructive? Would it be so self-destructive if they were actually committed to each other? Did she want to be committed to him? He'd soothed her after Andre had been killed. He might have come off as callous or arrogant, and he was those things, but he was also smart and fair and honest.

"I don't know how it would work, a relationship across worlds," she said.

"We'll make it work."

"I..." she was about to ask for time to think, but then she looked over the genie's shoulder and saw Dorian standing behind him. He'd taken up so much of her field of vision that she hadn't seen Dorian. His lips were pressed together, his pale cheeks splotchy.

The genie looked back and saw Dorian. "Just think about it."

Dorian thrust the kabob towards her without looking. The splotches on his cheeks grew an even deeper shade of florid crimson.

"You didn't get the genie one?" April asked. She'd meant it as a joke—obviously Dorian wouldn't have gotten the genie one—but she was so shocked at his reappearance that any mirth that might have been in her tone evaporated away before the words left her lips.

The genie sneered. "I wouldn't eat that overcooked street meat, anyway," he said. "If you wanted food, all you had to do was ask. I could have my personal chef prepare a feast fit for a queen." the genie's eyes blazed, burning away the vulnerability and tenderness he'd shown moments before.

Dorian took his kabob and walked up ahead of them without another word.

The genie watched him go triumphantly, but April shook her head in annoyance when he looked back at her. Her eyes must have betrayed her wrath, because his expression turned sheepish.

"Why do you look at me like that, sorceress?" the genie said.

April shook her hide, biting back the vile words in her throat. The genie didn't know any better—but was that really any excuse? "If this thing were to work out, you'd have to stop doing this."

"Doing what?" the genie said, genuine confusion blooming on his face.

"Being a jerk."

She stepped forward to follow Dorian, but the genie grabbed her wrist. "You said *if*—does that mean you're considering my proposal?"

"I don't know," she said, honestly. "Everything is happening very fast." The words made her feel like some hapless heroine in B-grade romantic comedy. She stared up into his eyes. Could she? She wasn't sure it was possible, yet telling him they were over seemed so final.

"I have to talk to Dorian." She pulled her hand free from his grasp, and he let it slip away.

She walked forward, Dorian nearly twenty paces ahead of her. She saw him stop to talk to a group of children dressed in tattered clothes. He handed them something. As she drew closer she saw what it was—the kabob. He hadn't taken a single bite out of it.

She looked down at her own skewer and sighed. She wasn't hungry any more, either. She wordlessly walked over to the kids and held it out. The oldest child reached out with one filthy hand and took it without thanks.

They walked a few minutes longer before Dorian began to slow. April hoped that he was going to stop and talk to her—maybe they could work this out—but he just paused, allowing the genie to walk up in front of them. Of course—he didn't know the way to the rot.

She also let the genie go up ahead of her, trying to find the words to say to Dorian. Before she could, he said, "Well, go on then. Follow him. I won't be far behind."

April felt her eyes prickle. She could tell he was hurt, but he was still trying not to be unkind. Oh, Dorian.

Not knowing what else to say, she started walking. They were almost there, anyway. After she'd walked for a few seconds she heard Dorian's even pace start up behind her, sand crunching beneath his leather boots and the cobblestone that lined the path between the buildings.

Finally they passed through the marketplace, coming out on the other side. The genie pointed to the corner. "There."

April nodded to it, not sure if Dorian and the genie were even talking at this point.

Dorian walked over to the rot. He bent down to get a closer look. He narrowed his eyes, then reached out his hand to touch the stuff.

"Don't," April warned, but he'd already laid the pad of one finger on the edge of the rot. Nothing happened.

"It's not spreading to you," April said. "It didn't spread to me or Thaddeus, either."

"That's because it's not ink rot," Dorian said, standing up. "At least not the parts around the edges." He pointed to the spiral pattern in the center she'd noticed earlier. "There's ink rot there, but it's underneath a layer of this ash-like stuff. It isn't very extensive; it's the amount you'd expect from what we saw on the cover the last time we checked. You could eradicate it right now without much problem, even without Thaddeus, if you could touch it. Unfortunately the ash has formed a protective barrier around it."

"If it's not ink rot, then what is it?"

"Magic of some sort."

"If it's just magic, then why did it appear on the cover of the book in the library?" April asked.

Dorian shrugged. "The ink rot itself is linked to the books. Some magic wielder would have piggybacked off that effect to make it show up. Must have taken a lot of work."

"But why would anyone do that?"

Dorian shrugged. "To draw us here, I'd imagine. Or, more accurately, draw *you* here."

Chapter 3

"What are you saying?" April said.

"Think about it," Dorian said. "There's only one person, one *magic wielder,* in this universe who even knows we exist. Only one who would have motivation to draw you here. Only one who uses fire magic." He turned to the genie, who stood a few feet away. "Him."

"That's ridiculous," April said, but the genie began to back away from them nervously.

"Of course it's ridiculous," he said, his tone unconvincing. His eyes darted back and forth between them, pausing on her before diverting back to Dorian.

April's heart sank. "You can't be serious. *You* did this? Just to get me here?"

The genie glanced between them one last time before sighing. He held up his hands in a gesture of surrender. "All right—you caught me. I never thought it would turn into such a drama. I thought you would come here alone and we'd have a warm reunion. There didn't seem to be any harm in it."

"You were trying to manipulate me," April said. "You *lied* to me."

"So what?" the genie said, sounding nervous. "I never sought to control you. How unfair is it that you can come and see me any time you please, but I have to wait like some pining street dog for you to show up?"

"How'd you do it?" Dorian asked.

The genie shrugged. "I tried several times to reach April magically, but nothing worked. Then I found this corner of rot—there *is* rot underneath the spell, like you said; it's just covered up by my magic. I remembered you telling me that you could see it in the library, and that's how you know where to go to fight it. I tried a few things before something finally worked."

"You never liked not being in control, did you?" April said. She couldn't believe that he'd gone through that much trouble to get her here. That in itself didn't harden her to the genie... but he'd lied to her even after she'd arrived, led her and her friends around on a wild goose chase, just to save face. "Were you ever going to tell me?"

The genie's expression grew angry. "At least I'm not like this love-sick fool."

Dorian crossed his arms. "I may be a fool, but I've never stooped to something as pathetic as this."

The genie's eyes flared. He waved his hand, and Dorian was thrown off his feet and against the stone wall behind him. It was like a wave of invisible energy had traveled from the genie's palm and into Dorian.

"Dorian!" April ran over to him. "Are you okay? Did you hit your head?" It hadn't been that long since William the Bold had knocked him unconscious. Another head injury could be disastrous.

"He's fine," the genie said, waving his hand dismissively. "I barely pushed him. I would not dare to seriously injure someone you deem a *friend*," the genie said. He emphasized the word friend.

"I'm fine," Dorian said. He took April's outstretched hand and allowed her to help him to his feet.

April whirled to face the genie. "What is wrong with you?"

"He said he's fine." The genie lifted his hand to wave dismissively again, but then his eyes widened.

His expression became panicked. He lifted his other hand to his eyes and examined it as well. "No, no no no no..." he muttered.

"What?" April said, her voice devoid of concern.

"My bonds have returned," he said, extending his wrists so she could see them. Two black lines in a swirling, interlocking pattern had appeared there, etched into the skin like tattoos, except blacker.

"But I am a free djinni," he said. "You freed me!"

April realized what happened. "I freed you on the condition that you never use your magic to harm anyone. You just harmed Dorian."

"I barely pushed him!" He crossed his arms. "Reverse it."

"What?"

"You freed me once, do it again. I barely pushed him. This is a mere technicality."

"Obviously, whatever's keeping track doesn't see it that way." She shrugged. "Come on, Dorian," she said. "Let's go back to the library. We'll deal with the ink rot later."

Fear registered in the genie's eyes. "You can't leave me like this."

Dorian shook his head. "As much as I wish we could leave, he has to remove the spell. It's encased the ink rot so that you can't touch it."

Damn it. "*Fine.*" She turned to the genie. "I release you from your bonds—again on the condition that you never harm anyone ever again. Good?"

The genie looked down at his wrists. The tattoos remained the same. His eyes widened. "The ring," he said. "You need the ring."

April placed her hand against her forehead. "I really don't have time for this," she said, with a sigh. "Where's the ring? I gave it to you, didn't I?"

The genie bit his lip. "Yes, you did."

"Great. Let's get this over with. And when we're done here, I never want to see you again. Where is it?" She spat out the words. They were mean, but he deserved them, didn't he, for what he'd done?

When the genie spoke, his voice was low, almost inaudible. "I don't have it."

"What do you mean you don't have it?" Dorian asked.

"I gave it away."

"Why?" April asked. "What if someone were to get ahold of it and use it to imprison you again?"

The genie shrugged. "You'd already freed me. It seemed redundant."

"*I freed you with stipulations,*" April hissed through her teeth.

"Stipulations I fully intended to follow. Why would I keep the ring around? It was just a reminder of my former captivity. I gave it to someone who would appreciate it."

"Who?"

The genie seemed reluctant to answer, but did anyway. "One of the girls."

"A prostitute?" April asked, "That's wonderful."

"For the record, I gave it to her before my feelings for you developed into what they are."

"Was that before or after we started sleeping together?" April shot at him.

The genie didn't answer, and it was all the confirmation she needed.

"Whatever," she said. "Not like it matters, anyway. Let's go find this girl and get that ring back."

~~~

"What do you mean, Zeinab doesn't work for me anymore?" the genie said. "Where could she possibly go that she would be treated as well as we treat her?"

They stood in the entrance hall of the House of Fire. The genie had dismissed everyone, including customers, except Asima when they'd entered. She stood in front of them, her arms crossed.

Asima raised an eyebrow at the genie. Unlike a lot of the genie's employees—April had always thought of them as groupies—she didn't seem as sycophantic. That's probably why she'd risen to a higher level of power than the rest.

"I don't know all the details. All I know is that she came in here yesterday all dressed up, trying to put on airs and doing a laughable job of it. Appears she suddenly came into a lot of money."

"Did she get a boyfriend? Did one of the patrons decide to make her his private courtesan?"

Asima scoffed. "Zeinab? Not likely, with her salty attitude. She sold something. Stole it from a customer, I'll bet. She'll be back here once the money runs out, which should be soon, considering how much time she's been spending at the Opium Room."

"Opium Room?" April asked.

"Oh, yes," Asima said. "Go there and get your fix, and be seen by everyone doing it. You can get your own private room and not remember a bit of it when you leave. That's what that fool girl has gone and done—paid the rent for a week, if you can believe it." She shook her head. "Enough money to feed the girls for a month."

April's mind flashed to the day the genie had talked her into sneaking into the magician's house and stealing his ring right off the man's finger. The magician had been so strung out on opium that she wasn't even sure if he'd known she was in the room.

The genie shook his head with disdain. "Opium. Like most addictive substances, you can dabble in it for a time before it fully ensnares you. Most never get the chance to fall into its trap. Only the rich can really afford to get addicted."

Dorian cleared his throat. "Sounds to me like we know where to go next." He turned to Asima. "Do you know the approximate location of this Opium Room?"

"I know where it is," the genie said. "I'll lead the way."

Dorian scowled, but didn't protest. They needed to get this done as soon as possible, and the genie would be with them anyway. He might as well make himself useful.

April nodded. "Fine, then."

The genie held her gaze for much longer than she was really comfortable with. His eyes conveyed a series of emotions both complex and contradictory. There was hurt there, and regret, but also pride. Did he really feel bad for what he'd done, or was he just embarrassed? He broke the eye contact without a word and walked out of the room. April nodded to Asima, who ignored the gesture, and they left.

"What do you think about all this?" April asked Dorian, glad to get a moment where they could speak in private.

"Too soon to tell," he said without meeting her gaze. He followed the genie out through the marble archway and into the bright sunlight. He was still upset with her. Well, he could take a number.

She pushed down the feelings if indignation growing within her. She didn't have time for them. They needed to get the genie's ring back so that he could reverse the magic blocking them from reaching the ink rot. And then they could get the hell out of here.

And never look back, April thought, trying to make herself believe in the finality of it. Despite all that had happened, she still couldn't imagine a world where she never saw the genie again.

~~~

"You've secured the finest quarters in the city, and still you live in squalor," the genie said in distaste, glancing around the room.

He wasn't wrong. The room was constructed with what looked like pink marble, the only example of the stuff that she'd seen in this world, and the archway was inlaid with jewels (too high up to reach, of course. It seemed the management didn't trust even its wealthiest clients.)

Yet that was overshadowed by the bedding and clothes lying in heaps on the floor, as though their owners had been spontaneously teleported off to some other dimension but their garments hadn't quite made the journey. Platters littered with greasy bones and half-eaten fruit were stacked on every available surface.

The former wearers of the forsaken garments lay sprawled across a bed, a woman and a man. Stained silk sheets were drawn up to their necks. It was a good thing, because they appeared to be naked underneath. The man was unconscious. He breathed heavily, his mouth hanging open—a side-effect of opium use that April recognized.

The woman, Zeinab, was awake, though she didn't look like she'd been that way for long. She must not have consumed as much opium as the man had. It was she that the genie addressed.

"I don't work for you no more," she said, her tanned face pouting. Despite the sour look, she was pretty, both her cheeks and eyes round and moon-like.

The genie raised his eyebrow skeptically. "Is this *specimen* the source of your sudden wealth?" he glanced down at the clothes littering the floor, picking one up with the toe of a satin slipper. "Unlikely. He wears the burlap clothes of a laborer. So tell me, how does a wench of poor breeding and circumstances such as yourself pay for a room such as this?"

"I don't work for you no more," she repeated. She smacked the man on the shoulder. "Wake up, Ahmed! Are you going to let him talk to me like that?"

Ahmed moaned but did not otherwise react.

Dorian sighed impatiently. "Just ask her where the ring is so we can get out of here. This place has an unfortunate odor." He wrinkled his nose at the stacks of platters.

"That's what I was going to do, obviously," the genie growled, unable to stand letting it appear that he'd let Dorian boss him around. He turned back to the girl. "The ring that I gave you," he said. "I need it back. Where is it?"

The girl's expression shifted from one of petulance to one of fear. She bit her lip. "Are you going to take back the gift you gave me?"

"That's the plan."

"Well I'm not just going to *give* it to you," she said. "It's mine, now. If you want it back you'll have to buy it. Not all of us can just throw away valuable trinkets like they're made of dirt."

The genie leaned in close to her, placing his hands on the end of the bed. "You want an offer? Here it is. Tell me where the ring is and I'll let you come back to work at the brothel once the cash that's paying for this place runs out—and by the looks of this room, that will be very, very soon."

The woman's mouth fell open, but she didn't respond right away. She glanced at Ahmed nervously. He continued to sleep as though they weren't even there.

"Don't look at him," the genie said, his voice suddenly loud, harsh. She yelped out of fear and surprise. "He will not save you after this is done. If you don't do as I say, I swear that not even the dirtiest, most flea-ridden whorehouse in the city will take you in—and you know what happens to those who work the streets unprotected."

"I didn't mean nothin'," the girl said. Her lower lip trembled. "I just wanted to have a little fun."

The genie's voice was suddenly gentle. "That's fine," he said. "Just tell me where the ring is and all will be well."

Her face screwed up, distorting her pretty features. She looked down at one of the stains on the bedspread. "I don't have it."

The genie's eyes flashed. When he spoke, he enunciated every word carefully. "What do you mean, you don't have it?"

"I sold it." She winced as the words left her mouth. "It's how I paid for this room, and all the opium and food."

The genie closed his eyes. "It's of utmost importance that you tell me where, when, and to whom you sold the ring." The words vibrated with tension.

"You'll let me come back?" she said. "You're right—I don't have much left. The money's running out faster than I thought it would."

"That depends on if I get my ring back or not," the genie said, and she winced. "So you'd better tell me what you know."

The girl couldn't get the words out fast enough. "There's a smoking room on the edge of the marketplace. The customer with the sideways eye—you know the guy—took me there a few days ago; I've been there with him before. I'm one of his favorites, you know. I was wearing your ring. I would have been more careful with it, but I never thought you'd give me something of actual value."

"I wouldn't, and I didn't," the genie said. "Go on."

"There was a man there—at least I think he was a man. He was the tallest person I ever saw—his head nearly touched the ceiling. He wore a cloak with a hood that fell so low it obscured his face. He saw me wearing the ring and asked if I would be willing to sell it. I said no, it was a gift, but then he offered me an amount of money I couldn't refuse. How was I to know you'd be askin' for it back, huh?" she looked up at April. "Tell me that if someone waved that kind of coin in your face, you wouldn't take it, no questions asked."

April winced. To be fair, she'd almost taken such a deal in order to try to treat Gram's cancer, back when she'd first found out about the gate. She didn't like seeing the parallels between the girl in front of her and herself, but they were there all the same. She couldn't blame Zeinab for taking advantage of an opportunity when it presented itself.

"What else do you know about this man?" the genie asked. "Remember, your future rests on me locating this ring."

She nodded. "I'm friends with the serving boy who works the smoke shop. He said he'd been coming in the last week, always sitting at the same table, always keeping his face covered. He didn't interact with anyone, not even the girls solicitin' for clients."

"Sounds like there's a good chance that he might be there today, then," April said.

The girl shrugged. "Maybe. I ain't been back. I took the money and got out of there. That's not the strangest thing, though." Her voice became quiet, strained. "When I took the sack of coin, I caught a glimpse of his hand. It was black."

"Black?" April asked. "How?"

"Frost bite can cause skin to turn black," Dorian mused. "But frost bite here? Doesn't seem likely."

"I don't know nothin' about that," the girl said. "I figured he'd been burned, or maybe he had some kind of disease—leprosy, likely. I didn't even count the money. I could tell by the weight that it was more than the ring was worth. I wrapped it in my shawl and left the ring on the table. I threw the whole package in the fire to burn any disease off. I only took the coins out of the flame one by one after the fire had burned down."

Leprosy? April shivered. She wondered if disease could be taken back through the portal. They'd need to be careful. She'd learned in school that many of the things people used to say about lepers were myths, but it was best to be cautious.

"We should go," Dorian said. "What if he's there now?"

They turned to leave, but Zeinab sat up straight. "What about me? I did as you asked."

The genie gave her a hard look. "Gather your things and go back to the house. Give any money you have remaining to Asima, and beg her for her forgiveness. It is her you need to worry about now, not me." He paused before turning back around. "Be gone before this man wakes up—and check his pockets. He's likely been stealing from you—that's why your money ran out so quickly."

They left, the girl's thanks echoing in the chamber behind them. They made their way out past the rooms full of motionless figures and into the sun.

April watched the genie moving up ahead of her. Why was he so inscrutable? He'd shown the girl mercy. Was that to save face with April, or did he really mean it?

She shook her head. It was so hard to tell sometimes.

"Do you think the man will be there?" she asked.

The genie's face was made of stone, hiding his worry. "I don't know."

"You really can't use your magic if you're bound to the ring?" she asked.

He shook his head. "While bound, I only have access to it if I'm commanded to use it." His face darkened. "I can only hope that this man doesn't know what he has. If so, he struck the deal of a lifetime when he bought that ring."

April nodded. She didn't want to say what she was thinking—that the man had bought the ring for a reason, and it probably wasn't that he thought it was pretty. The genie knew this without her saying it. They could only hope that the man didn't realize that the genie was again bound to the ring.

If he figured that out, they'd have an even bigger problem on their hands.

No one matching the description Zeinab had given was in the smoke room when they arrived.

"The last time I saw him was a few days ago," a boy holding a serving tray told them. "He came in every day for over a week before that. Always bought a single pipe of hash, but didn't say much. He spoke funny, so I assumed he was a foreigner. Never caused any trouble and overpaid. I figured he was here on business, and the business must have ended and he went back to his country."

"You weren't worried about the fact that he never showed his face?"

The boy shrugged. "Wasn't my concern. There are a lot of reasons someone wouldn't want his face seen. Maybe he was disfigured. What do I care if I don't have to look at it? I'd recognize him anywhere, though."

"How?"

"He was very tall. He had to duck down to step under that lamp, there." The boy nodded to a chandelier-like fixture suspended from the ceiling. Instead of lightbulbs, each of the arms held a small cup of oil with a lit wick protruding from it. The bottom of the chandelier dangled eighteen inches or so above April's head. She stood five feet, six inches tall, so that made the man's height nearly seven feet.

"You weren't kidding when you said he was tall," April commented. "Can you tell us anything else?"

"No, ma'am. And if you'll excuse me, I have tables to attend to." He left.

The genie looked defeated. Still, he pulled a silver coin from a bag on his hip and placed it on the tray. "Thank you for your time," he said. "If you see him again, send for me immediately at the House of Fire. There's more where this came from for you."

The boy's eyes grew wide as they fell on the tray. He nodded and pocketed the coin, looking left and right to make sure that no one saw that he'd had it. April didn't know how much a coin like that was worth, but it must be a lot.

The genie turned back to them, defeated. "I don't know what else to do."

"I don't, either." Even after all he'd done, April still felt sorry for the genie. He was living with a sword over his neck. How long would it be before the man figured out that the genie was his to command?

Dorian seemed to have no such worries, but at least he wasn't being cruel. "We should go back to the library. Perhaps Thaddeus can use the wand to remove the magic covering the ink rot."

"Would he know how?" April asked. In her experience, Thaddeus didn't know too much magic—his aversion to it, especially before he found out his mother was a witch, had prevented him from learning more than what was absolutely necessary when he was with The Collectors. When they'd been facing the ink rot, he'd only known a few offensive spells... maybe he'd known more, but knew they weren't strong enough.

"It's worth checking out," Dorian said.

The genie's eyes widened. "Wait—you mean you know someone who wields magic? Perhaps they could track the ring!"

"Maybe," April said.

Dorian sighed. "Whatever happens, we take care of the ink rot first. Got it?"

The genie nodded, eager to agree now that he had a shot of regaining his freedom.

No one spoke as they walked back to the gate. Dorian wasn't talking to her because he was still upset, and she wasn't talking to the genie because she was still angry with him. She'd expected him to be jabbering away, trying to regain her affection. But he remained silent.

She glanced at him. His face was full of tension, his lips pinched. He must be really worried. Of course he was—his freedom was on the line.

It serves him right, she thought to herself, but she didn't really feel it. She wished the genie hadn't done what he'd done, but she didn't revel in his misfortune—even if that misfortune was caused by his own arrogance.

"We're almost there." Dorian nodded up ahead.

April squinted. There it was—the building that the gate opened up to, a plain two-story structure fashioned from light brown adobe. It might have been an inn at one time, but now appeared abandoned.

"Thank goodness," she said, glad to get back to the library where at least she'd be able to speak with Gram and Thaddeus.

Jeez. Who could have predicted that she'd be happy to see *Thaddeus*?

Dorian's pace slowed, then stopped. He squinted in the direction of the door.

"What is it?" April asked.

"Someone's standing in front of the gate," Dorian said. He nodded toward a figure standing in the distance.

They were too far away to make out many details, but even at a distance she could tell that he was larger than the average-sized man, and thick, like a bodybuilder. He wore a cloak, the sleeves hanging past his fingertips, and the hood was down. He turned towards them. The place where his face should have been was dark, like a black hole sucking up the light.

"Is that him?" April asked. "The guy who bought the genie's ring?"

"Not many would wear a full cloak in this heat," Dorian said, "and even fewer of that stature."

"It's not a good sign that he sought us out," April said. She glanced at the genie. The only reason he'd follow them to the gate was if he knew the genie was again under the ring's influence and he'd come to claim his prize.

The genie looked back at her, his eyes wide, but she had more pressing matters to worry about than reassuring him. A woman across the street had ceased plucking the dead chicken in her hands, and had turned to watch them. The half-bald chicken dangled upside down from her hand, its head bobbing where its neck had been broken. Her unblinking eyes were vacant, an expression April was too familiar with.

She swatted Dorian's arm. "We've got UNCs," she said, the acronym for un-named characters—the people who populated a book but weren't main actors in its plot. They were harmless unless the main plotline of the story was threatened. In that case they turned into mindless zombies with one goal: *protect the story*.

"I'll handle it," Dorian said. He stepped forward, addressing the figure. "You've no doubt come to claim your prize—the control of this djinni." He paused for a moment, wavering. "Well, take him. He's been a thorn in our sides. We ask only that you command him to remove a bit of magic he laid that prevents us from finishing some work. Then we will leave you to your plans."

"Traitor!" the genie hissed, his eyes flashing and a wave of heat-like energy rolling off of him. He balled his fists, but was of course unable to do anything else.

"Dorian!" April said, shocked. "We can't just hand the genie over to him."

"Why not?" his eyes grew wide, hurt. "After all he's done you still protect him."

"I'm not protecting him. It's just not—"

"I suppose it's partially my fault. I encouraged you to see him."

"Dorian, don't do this."

Before Dorian could respond, the figure began to laugh, a sound that sent a shiver down April's spine. She turned towards the figure automatically, her Pagewalker instincts kicking in.

"What is it?" Dorian said, picking up on her reaction.

April didn't respond. Every ounce of her attention was being pushed towards the figure. Dorian's query was like background noise. Her heartrate began to rise. She hoped it was nothing...

"Who are you?" she called to the figure.

It laughed again. "You know who I am. Your gate has already told you. I can sense it."

The voice was wet, like someone with a bad cold speaking through a throat full of phlegm. But the liquid blocking this creature's vocal cords wasn't mucus.

"Show yourself," she commanded, her voice dry in stark contrast to that of the person in front of her.

"As you wish," the man said. He reached up—his hands *were* black; the girl hadn't been exaggerating about that—and pulled down his hood, revealing dark, glistening skin morphed into a mockery of a human face. Every feature in and of itself seemed normal, but together they didn't seem to fit. April couldn't articulate why; they were just *wrong*.

The creature's features glistened with the black of ink. The light refracted across its skin gave it a slight rainbow cast, like the shimmer of an oil spill.

"What is that?" the genie said.

"It's the ink monster," April said.

"I thought the ink monster was bigger?" Dorian asked. He must not be able to see the miniscule changes. Her Pagewalker senses must be granting her the ability to notice them.

"It was."

"I thought you'd *destroyed* it," Dorian said, his voice quivering like a violin string that's been tuned so tight that it's about to snap.

"I thought so, too," April said. "It doesn't make sense, but I'm *sure* that that is the same creature. I... I couldn't mistake that voice."

It was true. The first time she'd heard the ink monster speak, it had barely been able to form words, but the tone and timbre were unmistakable. It had bettered its speaking skills since then, but the sound of its voice sent the same chill through her heart.

"Bravo," the ink monster called. "I knew you'd recognize me! After all, we are old friends, you and I. 'Ink Monster,' though... the moniker lacks finesse. I was thinking of going by Hank Rottman. A sort of nod to Ms. Jackson, the woman who gave me my first title." As he spoke, a bubble of black blew out of his mouth, then exploded, sending dozens of tiny, night-colored spores into the air.

"How do you know about Mae?" Mae had been dead for months, long before they'd met the ink monster, let alone Hank Rottman. She glanced at Dorian, but he shook his head. This was news to him as well.

"I've met all of you, my dear. I know of your friend Randall, and his loyal hound, Rex. I've known the Victorian dandy standing next to you nearly as long as I knew Ms. Jackson. I even know your grandmother."

He cleared his throat, and more rot spewed forth from his mouth. "Of course, I didn't possess the faculties to really *assess* what I was seeing until very, very recently. I have you to thank for that—or perhaps your new friend Thaddeus. Mae and Dorian were only a force that sought to hold me back, destroying my progress in all but a few of the places where I grew. That seemed like enough for a while—I had many worlds to spread out in, even as they cut me out elsewhere, like the tribespeople *in Heart of Darkness* cutting back the edges of a jungle."

"What's he talking about?" the genie said from behind her.

April swallowed, loathe to say the words out loud. "He's the rot," she said.

"We already knew that he was connected to it," Dorian said.

April shook her head. "He's not just connected to it. He *is* it. It's like what we were talking about before: the rot is like giant mat of fungus or a hive of bees; it's all connected even if it doesn't look like it."

"But how does he know about Mae?"

"He remembers. He remembers everything." And they'd somehow set him free.

"Well, that's close enough," Rottman agreed with a shrug. "I wouldn't say I remember everything, exactly. I'd describe it as having access to those memories. Like a library." Another bubble had formed as he spoke, and he smiled, stretching it until it broke. More spores blew into the air. They floated towards the UNCs, who had multiplied since April last checked. "I hope you appreciate the analogy."

"What does he want?" the genie whispered so that Rottman couldn't hear him—though there was no way of knowing how sensitive his ears were.

"I don't know," April said.

Before she could say more, Rottman reached into the pocket of his cloak and pulled out a small object. She could barely make out what it was—but then he slipped it on his finger, the large red stone glinting in the sunlight above his knuckle. The genie's ring.

"Oh, no," the genie said. He turned and began to run.

He hadn't gotten more than a few steps when Rottman called after him. "As your master, I command you to stop!"

The genie stopped in his tracks, the upper half of his body moving forward slightly but his feet stuck to the ground.

"Teleport," April said to him.

He grimaced. "I can't." He swore in a language that April didn't understand. It sounded like the hiss of water on a hot stovetop.

Dorian grabbed her hand. "You can't help him, especially if we don't make it through that gate," he said. "You and Thaddeus together are the only ones who can stop him—if your hand holding trick even still works. He appears to be evolving to cope with different things, almost like a virus."

April nodded. He was right—she and Thaddeus had beat this creature once before—they could do it again. But first they had to get through the gate and to the other side.

Rottman certainly had time to intercept them, but he seemed to be barely paying attention. He was testing out his control of the genie.

"Turn around," Rottman said. April couldn't stop herself from glancing over her shoulder. The genie did as he was told, though his motions were jerky and reluctant. His expression was murderous, his eyes narrowed to tiny slits. His nostrils flared.

"By the fires of Allah," the genie said through clenched teeth, "You will regret this!"

"Not as much as you'll regret giving this ring to that empty-headed girl," the ink monster taunted. He still hadn't moved to stop them, even though they'd run past him. It looked like they'd be able to make it...

"Now, stop them from getting through that gate," Rottman said. April couldn't see his face, but she could hear the smirk coloring his voice.

She was still running full force when the genie materialized in front of them, a burst of smoke followed by flame. He appeared between them, and reached out and grabbed each of their wrists. She didn't even have time to slow down, and her arm nearly jerked out of her socket. Dorian grunted from the other side of the genie.

She tried to struggle, but the genie held her fast. "Don't fight me," he said, regret in his voice. "Don't make me hurt you."

His grip seared her skin like hot metal, and she struggled for several seconds before giving up. Dorian kept struggling for much longer.

Rottman stepped towards them, his face smug. For a second she thought his skin had actually become flesh-colored—but then it was gone as soon as it had appeared. A mirage.

"What do you want with us?" April asked.

"Nothing," Rottman said without looking at her. He addressed the genie. "In thirty seconds' time, destroy that building."

He nodded to the building that the gate had appeared in. At his words, the UNCs in the crowd began to hiss, and a ripple passed through them. This building being destroyed must interfere with the story somehow, or close to it. *Maybe they'll actually help us for once, rather than be a nuisance,* April thought, but then Rottman lifted his arm and wagged his finger at them.

"Nuh uh," he said. "We can't have you getting in the way. *As you were.*"

As though they'd been hypnotized and Rottman had just said the magic word, the UNCs all returned to their former activities. The woman April had seen earlier bent over and began plucking the feathers of the chicken again, as though unaware that she'd lost minutes of time.

April had only a moment to exchange a horrified look with Dorian before Rottman spoke again.

"The clock ticks, Djinni. You have your orders."

He mimed the bang of a mushroom cloud, then backed away towards the gate before disappearing through it.

"Genie, don't," April said desperately.

"I have no choice." The defeat and resignation in his voice scared her more than anything Rottman had said or done.

After a few seconds the genie released them, lifting his hands toward the building. He let out a guttural yell before wrenching his hands into fists, and the entire thing crumbled as though dynamite had been ignited beneath it.

Smoke and debris exploded into the air, forcing April to cover her eyes. She felt the abrasive bite of sand particles against her skin.

When the din settled, there was nothing left of the building except a mound of rubble. The gate was gone.

Chapter 4

"What's a grandmother to do, Thaddeus?" Gram said as she did crunches on the floor. She was enjoying the effects of whatever the genie had done to her. Thaddeus wasn't sure if he trusted the genie or not—he wasn't even sure if April trusted him, and she'd slept with him.

Gram continued speaking, a feat most able-bodied humans wouldn't be able to accomplish while doing Pilates without getting out of breath. She turned over and started doing push-ups.

"I mean, first she starts staying out late after work, and I'm left to wonder if she's involved in a drug or sex cult or something else unsavory. Wouldn't you feel relieved if you found out your granddaughter was out late not because of any of those nasty things, but because she found a boyfriend?"

"I suppose I would," Thaddeus said. "Though I've never had a daughter, let alone a granddaughter."

She nodded and kept talking. "Then I learn the reason she didn't want to go on a dream vacation with me is because she's become the guardian of a gate that allows you to go into books. At first it seemed like something out of a fairy tale, but every day it seems more and more the opposite. Ancient organizations? Magic that can take away a person's free will? Genies?" she paused. "I feel like I'm living in a work of fiction, myself."

"Those are all valid concerns. The gate and I don't have the best history. But..." he paused. "I have to admit it has its moments. It's been difficult to figure out how much of my distaste for magic is my own, and how much was brainwashed into me by The Agency." He shook his head.

"Exactly," Gram said. "And then these *men* start coming out of the woodwork." She'd started doing crunches again, and she suddenly stopped and sat up and looked at him. "Did anyone ever tell you that she brought that Barty boy over to my house and told me he was her boyfriend? But she didn't tell me his name was Barty, oh, no. She told me his name was Dorian! And before that, she told me that the man she was seeing was middle eastern. Well, I'll tell you what. There's not a single person more middle eastern then that genie!"

She lay back down and began lifting her legs in the air, doing reverse crunches. It was a move that Thaddeus remembered well from his daily training.

"Whatever that genie did to you seems effective."

"I suppose it is," Gram said, and she sounded slightly sad. "But don't think me some weak old woman. Before the cancer came back—heck, even after it came back—I could do this and more without breaking a sweat." Her expression grew troubled.

"Is everything all right?" Thaddeus asked.

She nodded slowly. "Like I said, this is the best I've felt in a long time, but... I can still feel the cancer. It's not gone, just suspended somehow. Does that make sense?"

"It does." Thaddeus often felt something similar with the gate. He felt normal most of the time, but it was always there beneath the surface. He could never tell when it would reveal its ugly side again.

Gram stood, and paced between two tables experimentally. "It is nice to be able to walk ten feet without wheezing," she said. "How long do you think this will last?"

"I don't know for sure," Thaddeus said. "But we can get an idea."

He stepped over to the lights and turned them off, then walked back. He pulled the wand out of his pocket and pointed it at her. He murmured a few words under his breath. As the last word of the incantation left his lips, Gram began to glow. The light seemed to be concentrated around her lungs, but almost all parts of her body exhibited a subtler glow. He could see the outlines of bones in places, and some blood vessels.

Gram looked down at her body in disbelief. Her eyes lingered on the brightest areas, the parts of her body most riddled with cancer. They needed the most magic to suppress her symptoms.

"My," she said, and then took a few more moments to get the next hoarse syllable out of her mouth. "My. I knew it had spread, but to see it..."

She fell silent.

Not sure what else to say, Thaddeus said, "The magic is bright. It should last for another hour or two."

He waved the wand and the light disappeared. He walked over and flipped the light switch on, and caught Gram wiping at the corners of her eyes.

"I'm sorry," he said. "I shouldn't have shown you that."

"No, I'm glad you did." She paused. "I've had a blessed life. But we always want more time, don't we?"

"Yes, we do."

They sat in silence for several more minutes, watching the activity on the other side of the shimmering veil. A goat bleated, sniffing at the doorway before scurrying off, its tail wiggling behind it. They laughed, both glad for the break in tension.

"Thaddeus?" Gram asked. She sounded unsure.

"Yes?"

"Do you think it was the wrong decision for me to start coming here? To keep going into the gate with April?"

"What else would you have done?"

"I don't know. Somehow kept her from this place."

Thaddeus snorted. "No offense, but I'm not sure anyone could stop her from doing something once she set her mind on it."

She sighed, suddenly seeming tired, even though her cheeks still held the rosiness the genie's touch had restored to them. "I was afraid of that. Thanks for listening to an old woman complain."

"Any time."

They sat in a companionable silence. If they'd met under different circumstances, Thaddeus thought they would have been good friends.

But something was bothering him. Had he forgotten something?

The hair on the back of his neck raised. It was like the gate was screaming at him, loud and completely silent at the same time. He moved to cover his ears with his hands, but of course that didn't help—it came from inside his head.

Gram's brow furrowed. "Thaddeus—is everything all right?"

He stood, lowering his arms to lower to his sides. He pulled the wand out of his pocket. "Something's happening."

She, too, stood. "What?"

"I don't know." He turned to the gate and she mirrored his stance.

"You should go home, now before the genie's touch wears off," he said, not sure what she would be fleeing from.

"No way."

"Are you any good in a fight?" He couldn't believe he was asking this of an old woman. They were lucky that the genie had given her his shot of magical adrenaline.

"I used to go to krav maga classes with April, plus kickboxing classes three times a week for five years."

He nodded. "It will have to do."

His attention was jerked towards the other side of the veil—as though the gate had grabbed his head and swiveled it in that direction. He almost shivered, thinking about the brief few minutes where the gate actually *had* controlled his body, but he loosed the thought from his mind. He didn't have time to think about that right now.

He held his wand at the ready, his gaze trained on the shimmering veil. A dark form stood on the other side.

Thaddeus heart stopped in his chest. Even though the figure was turned away from him, he knew immediately what it was.

"The ink monster," he said, his mind reeling. It wasn't possible. They'd killed it.

"Ink *what?*" Gram said. "Like ink rot?"

He nodded. "But worse."

The gate again forced his attention back to the other side of the veil. Behind the ink monster, two forms ran for the gate...

"That's Dorian and April," Gram said. "They're moving so fast."

"Time on the other side moves more quickly than over here." He'd never much noticed the effect—everything else they'd seen through the veil seemed to be moving at normal speed. Was it a perception issue, or because they knew April and Dorian, or because they were from this side? All questions for a less crucial time.

"We need to help them!" Gram moved towards the gate, but Thaddeus reached out and held his arm in front of her. He wasn't the one who did this—the gate did it.

"It's better if we stay on this side," he said.

"How could that be better?" she asked, her eyes miserable.

"I don't know... the gate told me. I think there's nothing we can do to help them."

He found himself rooting for them. *Come on!* He urged them forward with his thoughts like a man trying to influence the path of a ball after it leaves his fingertips. There was no way they'd be able to make it past the ink monster if he tried to stop them, or if he attempted to use the trick where he dissolved and moved across the ground and caught them...

But he didn't try to stop them. He didn't move at all when they passed. Was he not trying to keep them there?

His question was answered when, less than a second later, the figure turned and lifted its hand, revealing something on one of its fingers—a ring?

April and Dorian were less than fifteen feet away from the gate—*almost there*—when the figure pointed at them.

A puff of smoke and fire appeared in front of the gate. It dissipated, revealing the genie. He grabbed Dorian and April. They struggled but he held fast. His expression looked pained, as though he were holding them against his own will.

Thaddeus worked it out in his head. April had mentioned once that the genie had a ring rather than a lamp. The ink monster—now shaped more like a man than a monster—had the genie's ring. Thaddeus thought the genie was no longer bound to it, but that didn't appear to be the case.

He didn't have much time to puzzle over it, because the ink man had started to run towards the gate.

Chapter 5

Thaddeus had his wand at the ready. The creature moved through the gate, and as passed through, it slowed slightly, thanks to the time differential. Thaddeus took advantage of this. He spoke the incantation and the creature's feet froze in place, though his arms and body fought for release.

"Whatever you do, don't touch it," Thaddeus told Gram. Even though he didn't take his eyes off the monster, he saw her nod in his peripheral vision, showing that she understood.

"We've been here before, Thaddeus," the man-shaped creature said. His skin shimmered the rainbow tones of heat-treated metal.

His form had changed since the last time Thaddeus had seen him—by about fifteen feet. If you ignored the coloring, he looked almost human. He could easily pass for such at a distance at night, and even now in a fully-lit room, most people would probably not look at him closely enough to see that there was something wrong in the twist of his eyes, and the too-graceful, unsettling way he moved. He was like an android designed to look as human as possible—perfect in every aspect, but still not quite right as a whole.

"But I am different now, as you can see. Allow me to introduce myself: I am Hank Rottman." He bowed, a flourished gesture right at home in a Jane Austen novel.

"What do we do?" Gram said from beside him. Her voice quivered.

"We need to get him back on the other side. Then we need to retrieve April and Dorian."

"How—"

Before she could finish asking the question, the library rocked under their feet. The gate let out an immense shriek, so loud Thaddeus bent over with the pain of it.

"Thaddeus? What's happened to the gate? It's gone!"

She was right—the gate wasn't there anymore. The veil was still there, shimmering, as well as the arch, but the opening had been blocked by rubble. It was like looking at the inside of a door that had been bricked up from the outside.

Thaddeus shook his head, looking up again at the ink monster, Hank Rottman. His hold on the magic binding the monster had slipped, but the monster hadn't tried to move. Thaddeus reasserted the hold again.

"Very good, Thaddeus. I'm impressed. Last time you did that you would have lost concentration just for speaking. Now you only lost concentration when the gate let out its death shriek. Someone's been practicing."

Death shriek? Did that mean the gate was dead? No—Rottman was trying to manipulate him. He could feel the gate in the back of his mind. It was hurt, but far from dead. He wasn't even sure if it *could* die. The Agency had never actually destroyed any of the gates they'd collected, after all. Maybe greed wasn't the only reason for that. In any case, the gate was still alive—and it was angry.

Rottman was right about one thing, though: this holding spell was incredibly draining. He needed something that required less energy and concentration.

With a flick of his wrist, he morphed the holding spell into a vice around Rottman's arms, forcing the insides of his inky wrists to press together. It was like a pair of handcuffs, only stronger, no weak points or locks to pick. He did the same thing to Rottman's feet.

The spell wasn't as powerful as the full-body spell, and it gave Rottman more leeway. It never would have been enough to hold him when he was twenty feet tall. But Thaddeus would have to maintain only a small fraction of the concentration that he would for the more powerful spell. It was no longer a war of the wills.

Thaddeus pulled out a chair. "Sit."

Rottman did. As he walked, he left a trail of viscous footprints. Thaddeus' lip curled when he realized the prints were starting to ooze towards Rottman until they touched his foot and started to reincorporate into him. Rottman seemed oblivious to the amorphous puddle being slurped into his shoe. His eyes never leaving Thaddeus. Thaddeus didn't like the expression on his face. Why was he still smiling?

Movement from his side caught Thaddeus' attention. Gram, moving quick enough to almost be a blur in his peripheral vision thanks to the genie's touch, was moving towards Rottman, her hand outstretched as though to strike him.

"*How dare you* threaten my granddaughter!" she said.

"Gram, don't," Thaddeus said. He thought she'd make the strike before he was able to stop her, but he managed to take hold of her wrist before the blow fell on the man's face.

She turned to him, and for a moment he thought that she would turn that fear-fueled anger on him, but she didn't.

"If you touch him, you could become infected with the rot," he said. "April's not here to help you. Hell, I don't even know how the rot would act on this side of the gate."

He turned back towards Rottman. The creature's smile widened. That wasn't good.

Gram remained poised to strike despite his warning, but finally she pulled her hand out of his grip and let it fall to her side.

She turned on the monster. "I may not be able to cuff you, but mark my words—if you ever threaten my granddaughter again, you will not like the results. Do you understand?"

Rottman continued to grin. "I like her," he said to Thaddeus. "So much fire. You can see where April gets it." His next words were addressed to Gram. "You look better than the last time I saw you."

"What are you talking about? I think I'd remember meeting you."

"You've been accompanying the Pagewalker on some of her forays into my domain. You know—seeing the sights. Doing a little literary tourism?" he laughed at his own joke, and a three-inch bubble emerged from his mouth and popped, splattering tiny droplets on the floor and table. They immediately began rolling back to rejoin him.

"How do you know about that?" Thaddeus asked, narrowing his eyes at the monster.

"I was there. I'm in the corners of every world. Even as the Pagewalker destroys my limbs with her touch, I can't be banished for long. Even when you can't see me, I'm there."

"Don't listen to him," Thaddeus warned. "He's trying to get in our heads."

Gram nodded, but she leaned in to speak to him so that Rottman couldn't hear her whispered words. "But how did he know I was there? I've never seen this man before in my life—and I'd remember a face like that."

Thaddeus didn't nod, only met her eyes, hoping she'd understand that he acknowledged what she'd said.

"So you've managed to get into our world and block the entrance back to *One Thousand and One Nights*. You've taken ownership of the genie's ring, but how did you reverse his freedom?"

"He did that to himself." Rottman snickered. "I detected the verbal agreement that set the genie's conditional freedom immediately, and the inherent weakness it presented. Gaining access to the ring was easier than it should have been. His arrogance was his undoing. I thought I might have to coerce him into accidentally hurting someone—maybe attract an attack from him and then shift out of the way so that it hit someone standing behind me." He scoffed. "But all it took was some puppy love and a bit of jealousy. If literature explains anything, then it's how those who don't listen to warnings fall."

"What do you want? Why do all this?" Thaddeus asked.

"I simply want to be here. You know—see how the other side lives."

"Why?" Gram asked. "Why do you turn all those worlds black? Why destroy them?"

"Don't bother," Thaddeus said. "That's the same as asking a virus why it spreads disease. It doesn't have a reason. It just *does*."

"You're wrong," Rottman said, then he cocked his head in an almost-human gesture. "Maybe that's what I was like at first, before encountering Jekyll's serum. But wasn't that the same for every creature alive, including humans? Darwin's *Theory of Evolution* suggests so. Every creature started doing something just because—destroying the things around it for sustenance, reproducing, and then dying. The human race is the ultimate example of this. But the lucky get to evolve beyond that and find rewards greater than mere existence." He paused. "What do you consider your higher purpose?" Rottman did not wait for an answer. "Mine is to create."

"You don't create anything," Gram said to Rottman. "You only destroy."

The creature inclined his head slightly. "I suppose it could be taken that way. But from my perspective it appears that I am creating utopia."

"*Utopia?*" Gram scoffed. "Do you even know the definition of the word?"

"Utopia," Rottman said, speaking as though he were reciting a word in a spelling bee. "an imagined place or state of things in which everything is perfect. Antonym of *dystopia*. Utopia." He grinned. "That's according to the nineteen fifty-one edition of the Miriam-Webster Dictionary. Funny thing, it seems that the only place an "imaginary" world could exist in is a book. Such a funny situation, isn't it?"

"You have a skewed idea of what perfect means," Gram said. "April explained what it is that you do. You're a hateful, awful thing."

Afraid Gram might lose her temper, Thaddeus beckoned her over to him so that they could confer in private.

"Don't mind me," Rottman said. "I'll wait."

"What do we do?" she asked, her voice hoarse. "If the gate has been destroyed on the other side, how will April and Dorian get back?"

"It's not completely blocked," Thaddeus said. "Look."

He nodded to the gate, where spaghetti-thin streams of black ooze slipped between the cracks in the rubble. They fell to the floor as soon as they passed through the veil. *The door on the other side must be completely flat,* he thought.

"It's rejoining him," Gram said, revulsion in her voice. "So it's still open. But how are April and Dorian going to get through there?"

Thaddeus wracked his brain. "It's possible that we could enter via another page and meet up with them."

"So we have to find another page that describes the setting where they just were?" She wrinkled her brow, trying to wrap her head around it.

"That's the idea. It has to be on the same day they entered. Even if we enter on the other side of the city, we can traverse space if we need to. We can't, however, go back in time. Unless you have a time machine."

His mind sparked on the idea—April had used a time machine before. Could he do the same thing? He shook his head. There were too many working parts. It had been amazing that the Pagewalker and her friends had been able to make it work in the first place. He'd never be able to pull it off.

They'd need a bit of that Pagewalker luck right about now. Maybe being aligned with her would lend him some. He could only hope. He'd never been particularly lucky himself.

"What do you mean, time machine?" Gram asked, her eyes narrowed.

"I'll explain later." In any case, he'd at least need more hands than just himself. There was no telling when the genie's touch would wear off of Gram—and he had to keep control of Rottman. Damn it.

One step at a time. "Gram—read the pages immediately after the one they're in now—be sure to bookmark the page," Thaddeus directed.

"Going in after your friends?" Rottman grinned. "Don't worry about me. I'll be fine here."

"There's no way we're leaving you here alone," Thaddeus said.

"There's no way I'm going to go in willingly with you," Rottman said.

"Then I will force you in," Thaddeus growled.

"How?" Rottman asked simply. "I suppose you could use magic to make me go through the gate." He paused, waiting for Thaddeus to speak. When Thaddeus remained silent, he said, "That's what I thought. You've increased your command of the few spells you know, but haven't learned any new ones."

"What do we do?" Gram asked.

"First, we need to see if it's even possible to get to them," he said. "I need you to open the book to the next page—does this story continue?"

"Why wouldn't the story continue?" Gram asked. "There's so many pages left."

Thaddeus didn't know much about literature, but after the Agency's first encounter with the genie he'd read up on the book he originated from in case he met him again. "*One Thousand and One Nights* isn't like most books. It's the tale of a queen who will be killed by her husband on their wedding night, but she doesn't accept her demise willingly. Each night she tells the king a story, but doesn't finish it, so he has to let her live if he wants to hear the end. This scene is in *Aladdin and the Lamp,* one of the stories she tells."

Gram started to turn the page, then stopped, the edge of the page curled in her hand. "And if the story ends and a new one starts on the next page? What happens then?"

"We'll find a way. But we can't think about that, now. We have to take this one step at a time."

She nodded, the worried expression not leaving her face. She turned the page, and the gate groaned as it changed.

"What did I do?" Gram asked, her eyes moving towards the gate as though it might explode.

"It's okay," Thaddeus explained. "The gate does that if you switch between pages without closing the book first. It doesn't harm anything."

They glanced at the gate. It was still blocked by a pile of rubble.

"Try another page," Thaddeus said.

She turned the pages three times before a new scene appeared on the other side of the gate.

"Oh, thank god," Thaddeus said. Deep inside he'd been afraid that the gate itself was permanently damaged. If that were the case, he didn't know if they'd be able to get the others back—and then there were the implications of what would happen to the worlds if they were left unbalanced in the morning. "Is it in the same story? On the same day?"

Gram pulled her glasses off of the top of her head and read, her mouth moving wordlessly. She looked up at him and nodded.

"Smashing," Rottman said. "So you've found a way to reach them—but what about me?"

Thaddeus considered the creature's words, and had to admit they were right. They couldn't leave Rottman here alone, and there was no way to compel him through the gate. They were stuck.

Gram bit her lip. "I'll go by myself."

Thaddeus shook his head. "You're not well."

She did a kicking maneuver that she must have learned in one of the martial arts classes she'd attended with April, her foot striking the air a foot in front of her face. "I feel fine."

"Thanks to the genie's touch! Who knows how long that effect will last?"

Gram hooked her thumb in Rottman's direction. "He's right. You can't go, and you can't make him go. It's our only option."

"We could call Randall," Thaddeus said.

"Randall will have already caught the last bus. With the time differential, who knows how long that will be for April and Dorian? Getting to him will take time we don't have."

No matter which way Thaddeus spun it around in his head, she was right. She was the only one who could go and find them.

"But the genie," Thaddeus said, grasping for a reason that she couldn't go. "It's too dangerous."

"The ring controls the genie, right?" Gram said. "Well, looks to me like we've got the ring right here." She pointed at Rottman, who smiled at them as though watching an interesting debate, rather than a conversation that would decide his fate.

"How are you going to get it off of him?" Thaddeus said.

"He's right," Rottman said with that thin, wide smile. "Even if you could take it off my hand, it's covered in rot. You can't get it without getting a little of me on you."

Gram thought for a minute, and then nodded slightly as though coming to a decision. She walked over to Rottman and reached for the ring.

Wait—" Thaddeus said, but he was too late late.

Rottman didn't struggle, but the ink around his hand shifted as though to escape Gram's touch. She was able to grasp it, but pulled it through his fingers rather than off of them. It made a sound like a stuck shoe being pulled from mud. Some of the goo stuck to her fingers. "Well, then I'll just have to find April as soon as possible, won't I?"

Rottman's eyes narrowed, but the show of annoyance was only momentary. Within a second, the grin was back on his face. "Tricky," he said, the words wet and phlegmy. "You really are just as bad as your granddaughter."

"Because I raised her right," she said in a no-nonsense tone. "Now hush, you." She held the ring up so she could examine it. It *was* covered in rot; the red stone nearly obscured. Her hand wasn't much better. Some of the black goo that had come off with the ring had started to slide down her wrist and plop down onto the floor in an effort to reunite with Rottman, but not all of it. A black tinge stained her palm and around her nails. She slipped the ring on her finger.

Thaddeus closed his eyes and sighed, resigned. "You're really doing this, then?"

She raised her hand, showing the splotches of black. "Looks like we don't have a choice."

"You also don't have much time," Rottman quipped.

Thaddeus didn't verbally acknowledge Rottman's words. Instead he moved to stand between him and Gram so that she couldn't see him. "He's right," he said, his voice low, though Rottman could undoubtedly still hear. "You must leave *now*." Thaddeus strode quickly towards the gate, and she followed. "How do you plan to find them? Or did you think that far?"

"The genie said to ask for him at the House of Fire. I'll start there."

Thaddeus nodded. "Remember, the command must be verbal, and the genie has to be able to see you when you give it. Do it as soon as you see him.

He's compelled to enact Rottman's commands until you give your first. Understand?"

She nodded.

"After you're in, I'll reopen the book to the page where the gate was destroyed. Assuming you're successful, you should be able to command the genie to fix the damage he caused—he can do it, I've seen his power firsthand." He placed his hands gently on each of her shoulders to make sure she paid attention to what he said next. "You'll feel it when the magic starts to wear off. It will happen gradually but quickly once it starts. As soon as you feel the tiniest hint of weakness, you get back here. Not only for yourself, but for both our worlds' sakes. Understand?"

She paused, considering his words. Then she nodded.

"Better hurry." Rottman leered at her from over Thaddeus' shoulder. "The fire of the djinn's touch won't burn forever."

"Ignore him." Thaddeus held her gaze until he was satisfied that she hadn't been ruffled. "I'll check this page periodically to see if you're here. Good luck."

She stepped backwards and through the veil. Thaddeus watched as her back receded through the veil, moving suddenly much quicker, like she was being fast-forwarded.

"Looks like it's just you and me," Rottman's voice said from behind him.

As Thaddeus turned back, the skin of Rottman's face and hands appeared flesh-toned. Thaddeus did a double take. The second time he looked, Rottman was his usual inky-black self.

Rottman smiled. "What's wrong, Thaddeus?"

Thaddeus hid his trepidation. He didn't want Rottman to see that he was spooked.

"I thought I saw something," he said.

Rottman's smile widened. "Must have been a trick of the light."

Chapter 6

Dorian stared at the pile of rubble where the gate had been, stunned. "Is it..." he didn't finish the sentence. Dorian had spent many years protecting the gate. For it to suddenly get destroyed would be a devastating blow for him.

"It's still there," April said. "I can feel it. It's just blocked."

"You need to leave now."

April turned towards the genie, the source of the words. The genie wasn't currently attacking them—instead he stared down at his hands as though confused by them. Still, they couldn't trust him.

He looked up. "He only commanded me to keep you from the gate, but it's safest for you not to be around me."

April didn't argue. He was right.

"We'll be back." She backed away from him. Dorian followed suit. April's eyes never leaving his until Dorian pulled her around the corner.

"Would you stop making eyes at him? He just trapped us here!" Dorian said angrily. "And we wouldn't be in this mess in the first place if he just communicated with you like a normal person."

"You're one to talk," April muttered. To her surprise, Dorian heard her.

"What's that supposed to mean?"

April shook her head. They didn't have time for this. "Never mind. Is it possible to destroy a gate by destroying the door that it opens up to?"

"I wouldn't know," he said. "I've never seen this before. In all my years working with Mae, nothing like *any* of the things that happen with you ever happened!"

"Why are you yelling at me?"

Dorian sighed and closed his eyes. "I'm sorry. This is just very stressful."

April let several moments of silence pass before speaking again. "Do you *think* that this could have damaged the gate?" She could feel the gate below the rubble, it was alive, but stunned from the blow. What if the stunned condition was permanent?

Dorian sighed. "As far as I know, the gate works like the doors of an adjoining room. You can see this in everyday use—if there's a door on this side, then we have to open it before we can step through. That's just speculation on my part. Or maybe wishful thinking."

"Okay, but what if one of the adjoining rooms is completely destroyed?" April asked.

"It should be the same—what happens over here shouldn't affect what's happened over there."

"Shouldn't," April repeated flatly. Was that really all they had to go on? Despite all that Dorian had said about adjoining doors and one side not affecting the other, she knew that if a bomb was set off in one room the other door, and probably the room, as well, would have been destroyed.

Oh, God. What if the building coming down had somehow affected the library? Gram and Thaddeus were over there. Thank God Randall was at his orientation.

Damn it. Why had she ever thought it would be okay to involve Gram? She should have left her at home where it was safe, where the only thing she had to worry about was April staying up late to spend time with her boyfriend.

She shook her head. The gate should have held back the blast, or at least most of it. And why would Rottman go through the gate if the other side was destroyed? That gave her a little hope.

"So how do we get out of here?" April asked. Not only did they need to get back to Gram and Thaddeus, they were up against a time limit. If they were still in the world of *One Thousand and One Nights* when the gate's connection severed at five, both this world and theirs faced destruction.

But Rottman would know that, right? Maybe he didn't care. He had so many other books to run amok in, losing one wouldn't make a difference.

"I can see two options available to us," Dorian said. "The first is we get over to where the gate was and check if it's still possible to pass through."

"But the genie is there," April said. "You heard him—he won't let us anywhere near it."

April shivered, remembering the acts of power she'd seen the genie perform. He'd always produced them so easily that she was sure he was showing only a small fraction of his power. "What's the second option?"

"Hope the others realize what's happened and open to a different page."

"That's it? Just *wait?*"

Dorian nodded. "It gets worse—they have to deal with Rottman first. If he caught them by surprise..."

April shivered. If Thaddeus got hurt it would be bad enough, but if Rottman harmed Gram...

"What does Rottman want? Why would he want to go to our world?"

"I don't know. But it's not good."

She bit her lip. "There's a third option. We fight the genie."

"How?"

"We fight fire with fire. We get another genie."

Dorian started to protest, but his mouth closed as he thought it over. "The magician."

~~~

They made their way in the direction that April *hoped* would lead them to the Magician's residence. She'd only been there once and had been disoriented at the time. The genie tried to steer clear of the area where the magician lived, or at least that's what she assumed. He'd never brought her there. She once asked him why, and he said because he'd be tempted to break her no-injuring-others condition.

Luckily, her Pagewalker senses guided her. Each time she thought that maybe she'd taken a wrong turn, she'd notice something else she recognized from the one other time she'd taken this path—it was almost like the gate was highlighting them.

Finally they came upon a familiar courtyard centered around a well. A clay pot attached to a rope leaned against the clay bricks that formed the low circular wall around the shaft.

"That's the well where I stopped to rest the first time I came here," she said. "This is the place."

"Are you sure? There must be dozens of wells just like that around the city."

"I'm sure."

From the look on Dorian's face he wasn't willing to trust her instincts. Usually he didn't question her, but he was in bad mood.

The door of a nearby house opened and a middle-aged woman stepped out.

"Fatima!" April squealed, running up to the woman. She was so happy to see her, because she proved that this *was* the right well, that she'd forgotten how unpleasant the woman had been.

Fatima rested the clay pot she was carrying on her hip and squinted up at April.

"Who are you?" she said. "If you're one of the new brides, you should know I won't be able to remember all your names. And it's not good to approach an elder." Her chest puffed up. "You don't want to get a bad reputation, do you?"

April immediately regretted approaching the woman. She opened her mouth to respond, but Dorian walked forward, cutting her off.

"Forgive my sister," he said. "We are coming to visit our uncle. He's spoken of you many times. She simply forgot her manners."

Fatima's eyes narrowed even further. "Uncle? What's his name?"

Uh oh. They didn't know the magician's name.

"He lives in that house over there," Dorian said, pointing at the house where she'd found the genie guarding the last time she'd been here.

Fatima's eyes widened when she followed Dorian's finger. "The magician is your uncle?"

Dorian nodded. "Perhaps you'd like to come and talk to him?"

She stepped away from Dorian, nervous. "No, no. That won't be necessary." She paused, then spoke again. "I don't know why your uncle has seen it fit to have my name in his mouth, but whatever offense I have caused, please offer him my sincerest apologies."

She lowered her head in a bow-like gesture and backed away. She receded back into her home without filling her pot. April thought she heard the slam of a wooden bar being dropped on the other side of the door—an old but effective version of a lock, she supposed.

"Don't mess with the magician," April said.

"She's probably inside doing some sort of counter-curse," Dorian said. "Kitchen sink magic, like tossing salt over your shoulder to ward off bad luck. It'll keep her busy for a while. Come on."

They walked over to the magician's door. April pushed on it. It didn't give.

"Locked," she said.

Dorian peered through one of the windows. The window wasn't covered with glass, but with a thin sheet of solid marble that had an intricate lattice design carved into it to form a screen. The House of Fire had similar screens on their windows. The genie had told her that they would throw water on them during the hottest days and it would cool the entire building.

"I don't see him. He could be in another room."

Dorian suddenly turned, moving to stand with his back pressed flat against the wall of the building, as though he didn't want to be seen from the inside.

"What?" she hissed, on high alert.

"Someone moved into the room. I don't know if they saw me."

The door vibrated as the latch on the other side of the door was lifted.

"I think they saw you," she said.

A moment later the door was thrown open. A man April had never seen before stepped out. April had been expecting the magician, but this man was younger, with dark skin and light-colored eyes.

"What are you doing out here?" the man said. He crossed his arms in front of his chest.

"We're looking for the magician." April glanced at Dorian, hoping that he'd have something to add, but he looked as lost as she felt.

"What business do you have with him?"

April faltered. "It's a private matter."

The man considered her words for a moment, then shrugged. "You'll have to come back later with your request. He's away."

He moved to close the door, and as he did April saw the chain-like tattoos on his wrist.

"Wait," she said, placing her hand on the door to stop him from closing it. "You're a djinni?"

His jaw hardened. "Yes. So you should know that I have powerful magic and should not be annoyed."

"I know those chains on your wrist mean you can't do any magic, powerful or not, without an order from your master."

The djinni's expression grew furious. "He's given me leave to protect his house from the ne'er-do-wells of this neighborhood," he said. "And I'm starting to suspect that's what you are." He looked at her for the first time straight-on, and his eyes widened. "You're the one who snuck in here and freed the djinni of the red ring."

"Djinni of the red ring?" Her genie's ring was red. "Don't you know his name?"

"Djinn do not share their names, except among the closest of family and friends. Probably not even then. A name is a great source of power and control."

"Seems like control is something you've already lost," April said.

His face was suddenly less than an inch away from hers, his teeth bared. He couldn't use his magic to hurt her, or at least she didn't think he could, but he was still much larger than he was.

"I mean no offense," she said, taking an unconscious step back before steadying herself. "But you're right. I'm the one who freed the genie—I mean, the djinni of the red ring. What if I freed you, too?"

The djinni laughed. "You can't. Even if that inebriated fool hadn't started taking precautions, he isn't home right now."

"Right." April thought fast. "But I still know the djinni of the red ring. We're close, actually. I could get *him* to come free you."

"He's been free for months now. If he was going to save us he would have done so already. Why should I believe that he'd come back to free me just because you tell him to?"

"He's got himself into some trouble," April said. "I freed him from his ring the first time, but he broke the promise he made to me. He's under the ring's influence again. When I free him this time, I'll make it one of the conditions that he must help you."

The djinni gripped his chin, considering her words. "That could work. But, why should I trust *you?*"

April thought for a moment, but Dorian spoke before she could find the right words.

"You don't have anything to lose by trusting us. Even if we don't keep our end of the bargain, you're no worse off. You might as well take the chance."

The djinni nodded his approval. "And do you plan to cause the magician harm? Steal his property? Destroy his residence?"

"Well, *one* of those things," April said, hoping honesty was the best policy.

"Good. That alone is worth letting you pass. He did command me to protect his home from local troublemakers. Lucky for you, you're not local, though I do hope you'll make some trouble. Come."

He stepped away from the entrance and let them pass.

They stepped into the house. Even though several lamps and candles were lit inside, it was dim after standing out in the sun. The cloyingly sweet scent of opium oil clung to the walls, but wasn't as strong as the first time she'd been here.

She'd gotten some of the stuff on her hands, and hadn't been able to get rid of the smell for weeks. She hadn't been a huge fan of poppies before that, but now she couldn't stand them. She'd recognize that scent anywhere.

"I must continue to guard the house," the djinni said. "Remember, tell the djinni of the red ring that he must free the genie of the cobalt ring—not sapphire, not diamond, not blue. *Cobalt.*"

"Cobalt, got it," April said. The djinni went and stood in front of the lattice window, looking out at the street. April wondered if he'd tell them if the magician came home. Maybe, but she wouldn't bet on it. He seemed like he would just as happily enjoy the entertainment of whatever the magician would do to them if he found them. He didn't seem that confident that the "djinni of the red ring" would actually help him.

"Where to now?" Dorian hissed at her.

She looked around, then realized the problem. "The magician's not here. He's wearing the rings," she said. How would they get the rings when they were on his fingers?

"Great," Dorian said.

"Hold on," April said. "Let's not give up yet. Maybe he left some behind. His fingers were *really* full of rings when I saw him, so if he had more than that there was no way that he could wear all of them."

"Do you really think a man would leave something as powerful as a genie's ring unguarded?"

"It *is* guarded." April nodded to the cobalt djinni.

"But we managed to get in here."

"On a technicality. Come on—we have to at least look."

They poked around the house, the cobalt djinni watching them with an amused expression on his face.

Yetch. Were *all* djinn like this? Maybe she'd judged her genie too harshly. It was probably all he'd ever known.

Her cheeks became suddenly warm at the idea of *her* genie, even though she'd only thought the word. She was glad that it was dark in here and Dorian couldn't see her. Not that she thought he'd notice. He hadn't looked at her any more than he'd needed to.

Every room was filled with beautiful things, but all of them were either too large to move or obviously not worth that much. She was about to give up hope when she passed through a curtain and into a small room.

Due to the lush furnishings, she was sure that this was the magician's private chamber. A wooden table held a vial of what must have been a travel-sized bottle of opium (*TSA compliant,* she thought wryly) and various toiletries, including a hairbrush and small knife.

And a box. Her eyes moved over it, onto the hairbrush, which was much more interesting...

She turned away and blinked. Why was she suddenly tired, her vision blurry? She'd been fine just a moment ago.

She moved to find Dorian, who had gone to search a separate part of the house. This was a waste of time. They'd have to find something else to fight the genie with, because this was a dead end.

But something made her pause. The gate's voice in her head urged her, *look again. This is important.* She turned back to the table. She'd already looked there and found nothing, but still the gate insisted.

She began picking up objects and examining them. Were they spelled to appear different, glamoured?

The fourth or fifth time her eyes scanned over the table that she realized that she hadn't bothered to open the box that sat unassumingly behind all the other objects.

But why open the box? It was unimportant, barely worth looking at. It was so nondescript she had a hard time noting its dimensions and description. It was small enough to fit on the table, but anything beyond that slipped into her brain and out again like water through a sieve.

The soft *tap* of Dorian's shoes on the rug-covered floor drew her attention.

"I didn't find anything," he said. "Did you have any luck?"

"No, but... come here."

He walked over and stood next to her, looking down at the table.

"A man's vanity kit," Dorian said. "So what?"

"Not that," April said. "That plain wooden box in the middle."

"What box?" his brow furrowed as he looked for it, almost as though it blended into the table. "That? What about it?"

"I think it's glamoured."

He squinted, then his eyes widened. "I think you may be right."

April reached out. The gate pointing out the box had made her able to focus on it slightly more, and talking with Dorian about it had increased the effect. She was now able to hold it in her field of vision, even though her eyes blurred out of focus as she did so.

She reached out and felt the box, half-expecting for it to be trapped—but why would someone bother to glamour a box that was booby-trapped?

Unable to see clearly, she fumbled with the lid until she was able to unhinge the plain clasp holding it closed. The wood was rough, unfinished. A good choice—no one would expect anything of value to be stored in a box like this one.

As soon as the lid was separated from its lower half the box came into focus. Inside were a series of small objects. Pieces of wood and what looked like bones and small off-white nubs—teeth, she realized. Ick. She hoped to never know what they came from, let alone what they were used for. Nestled in one corner was a small ring.

"Bingo," She reached for the ring.

"Don't touch anything else in the box," Dorian warned. "We don't know if any of it's hexed."

She nodded. The ring touched a yellowed tooth, and to pull it out she had to extend her pinky as though drinking a cup of tea and insert it through the ring. She hooked her hand slightly and the ring came with it.

"Got it," she said.

The ring was fashioned from silver, with a filigree pattern running along the band that reminded April of the pattern she'd seen on the genie's wrists. The stone was half the size of her pinky nail and purple-blue.

"Are you sure that's a djinni ring?" Dorian asked. "Why would he leave this one behind when he took the rest with him?"

"See that chain-like pattern? It's definitely a djinni ring. I have no idea why he'd leave it behind, but I'm not going to look a gift horse in the mouth. It's almost too small for *my* little finger. Maybe he wasn't able to wear it."

"Fine," Dorian said. "We'll summon the djinni once we get back to the gate. No point in suffering another narcissist on the way."

They passed out the way they came in. The cobalt genie looked down at the ring as they did. His mouth spread into a wide grin that revealed perfectly white, though slightly sharp, teeth.

"Remember our bargain... *if* you're able to best the djinni of the red ring."

Then he laughed. It didn't seem like a good sign at all.

Chapter 7

"Can you tell me where the House of Fire is?" Gram had lost count of the number of times she'd spoken the question; the words had all but lost their meaning. Perhaps it was rude in this culture to stop people and ask for directions, because every person she asked gave her a dirty look and walked away.

She was just about to give up hope when she was approached by an older woman with sympathetic eyes.

"You seek the House of Fire?" she asked.

Gram nodded, hope igniting in her chest. "Yes. Do you know where it is?"

The woman's eyebrows knitted together. "All these people are wondering what a woman such as yourself could possibly want with the House of Fire." She paused, then lowered her voice. "Are you trying to find a loved one?"

Gram nodded, thankful for the woman's kindness. "Yes, my granddaughter."

The woman's expression became grave, and she nodded knowingly. "I knew it as soon as I saw you—you are looking for someone. My cousin's daughter met a similar fate. It is a terrible thing."

"Uh, yes," Gram said. She had no idea what the woman was talking about, but she didn't want to anger the one person who'd agreed to speak with her. "Can you point me in the right direction?"

The woman nodded at a nearby side-street. "Follow that road for ten minutes. You can't miss the women standing outside. Do not tell anyone how you found its location. My family's reputation is tarnished enough."

She turned to leave, but Gram gripped her hand. "Thank you," she said, hoping that the woman felt the sincerity if her words.

The woman seemed surprised, but she squeezed Gram's hand. "Good luck—and take consolation that she's at the House of Fire. I hear they're treated well there."

She glanced down at Gram's hand, where the ring was visible on the middle finger of her right hand. The ink rot wound its way down around the base of her middle finger and through the webbing of her thumb—luckily the woman hadn't come into contact with it. Gram swallowed. She needed to be more careful.

Gram expected the woman to ask about the rot, or perhaps recoil from it, but she didn't. In fact, she didn't seem to notice it at all. She only commented on the ring. "Is that ring how you plan to buy her freedom?"

Gram nodded, not sure what she meant by freedom.

"Good. Keep it hidden."

She turned away, her eyes darting around as though checking who had seen her. She carefully pulled her scarf back over her face so that only her hooded eyes remained visible.

Gram followed the woman's directions, walking as quickly as possible. Thaddeus' warning about the genie's touch wearing off rang in her ears. She had to hurry. She hadn't felt this fit in years, but it wouldn't last.

She heard the giggles before she saw the young women leaning against a marble building that stood out from its nondescript neighbors, thanks to the decorative arches. The women were dressed in colorful silks, and showed far more skin than any of the women Gram had passed so far. They were hardly scantily clad by modern ideals, but they probably were by the standards of the world they were in.

Gram looked around her. She'd been so caught up in her own thoughts that she hadn't noticed the crowd thinning out, or that every person walking down this particular street was a man. The colorfully-dressed women shot her concerned looks, but they addressed only the men, speaking in soft, purring voices.

"Oh," Gram said, finally realizing what was going on. "*Oh.*"

Of course this was a brothel. The conversation with the woman now made so much more sense.

She waited for the men to enter the House of Fire—that's what they were here for, wasn't it? But they stood outside awkwardly. Some shot her furtive glances.

Well, then she'd have to be the one to act. She lifted her chin—she'd once petitioned the city council to have a traffic light installed on their street. They'd written her off at first as a meek suburban grandmother, but she'd made them listen, hadn't she?

The women glanced over in her direction. One leaned through an archway, speaking with someone inside. A few moments later another woman stepped out—no, not a woman, a girl.

Heavens, Gram thought, *she looks barely fourteen!* She supposed children had to grow up faster here.

The woman spoke to the girl for a moment, then the girl nodded and stepped over towards Gram. As she approached, Gram realized that she wasn't dressed as provocatively as the others. She also had dirt under her fingernails and clutched a wet rag. She wasn't a prostitute; more likely a cleaning girl. Gram breathed a sigh—it was a good thing, too, because the closer she got, the younger the girl seemed.

"Please, Ma'am," the girl said, her tone too adult for her age, "Just go. You're affecting business." She twisted the rag nervously in her hands as she spoke.

"There seem to be plenty of customers." She nodded towards the men leaning against the walls on the opposite side of the alley. None of them were interacting with each other, or looking at the women or the brothel at all. One glanced up furtively at her, but for the most part they kept their faces turned away.

"They do not want to insult a woman of your age and standing by engaging with us in your presence," the girl explained. "Please leave. We do not bother anyone here, and the brothel's owner donates money to the upkeep of the city every month."

Gram wondered who she was disguised as that she was causing so much trouble. She knew that the gate disguised anyone who stepped through it as someone who blended in on the other side. She hadn't stopped to check what she looked like. She hadn't wanted to waste the time.

"I mean no trouble," Gram said. "It's because of this building's owner that I'm here. He once told me that if I was ever in this part of town, I only had to ask for him here."

The girl's brow furrowed. "*You* know the djinni? How?"

Gram gave the easiest explanation she could. "He knows my granddaughter."

The girl shook her head in disbelief. "No girl who grandmother wears silks as fine as yours would work here. And if she did, her family would disown her. Especially someone such as yourself."

Gram again wondered what the gate had disguised her as. A rich old woman with a stick up her butt? It wasn't any of her concern what these women did—though she had a hard time keeping the same open mind for this girl, who appeared so much younger than all the other women standing out on the street.

"What's your name?" Gram asked.

The girl shrugged. "Rhea."

Gram noticed that the other women were now giving her dirty looks, some with their arms crossed. One even tapped her toe impatiently. One or two of them must have slipped inside the building while she was speaking with the girl, because two of the women who had been outside before were now walking out through the doorway with a third. The new woman was slightly older than the others, though not by much.

Rhea suddenly seemed nervous, as though she were afraid of the new woman. "I tried to get her to go away, Asima, but she wouldn't listen—" she seemed ready to say more, but fell silent when Asima fixed her with a sharp stare.

"What is the issue?" Asima asked, the question directed at Gram. Her lips were pressed into a thin, disapproving line.

"There is no problem," Gram said. "I'm simply looking for my granddaughter."

The woman raised an eyebrow. "Your concern for your kin—or more likely your reputation—is endearing, but your granddaughter is not being kept here against her will. All of our girls choose to work here, and they are all of age to make such decisions for themselves."

"Even this one?" Gram asked incredulously, nodding towards the girl. "She's so young."

"Rhea is of age," the woman said, "though she looks younger. Some would consider that an advantage in our line of work. However, the genie chooses to keep her as a cleaning girl until she's older."

The girl—Rhea—lifted her chin proudly. "I'm sixteen," she said. She looked fourteen at best, in Gram' estimation. Maybe she was lying, or maybe she'd been undernourished as a child and looked younger because of it.

"That's hardly an adult," Gram protested.

Rhea laughed. "My cousins, younger even than me, are all married. And you think that I'm not an adult?"

Gram sputtered for a moment before she got her expression under control again. She knew better to judge another culture's norms, especially one that had existed so long ago, but knowing what these children—women—were doing had taken her by surprise.

Asima's eyes narrowed. "You seem ignorant of our customs. What is your granddaughter's name?"

"April," Gram said, and Asima's eyebrows raised in recognition.

"She says she knows the djinni," Rhea added, her tone implying that the suggestion was laughable. "Isn't that funny?"

"Rhea, back to work. The courtyard needs sweeping."

Rhea looked indignant at the insinuation that she was dawdling on purpose. "She was scaring off the customers!"

Asima gave her a stern look and she fell silent, averting her eyes from the sharp gaze.

Asima's eyes lost none of their sharpness when she turned them on Gram. "Follow me inside before you completely kill my business with your presence. Come."

Gram did as she was told. She glanced back at the men standing on the opposite side of the alley. They watched her carefully, their eyes widening as she entered the building. She wondered what they thought she was doing. Did they think she was here as a patron? Or that she worked here?

Both seemed equally laughable, and she cracked a smile. Maybe she'd do a little turn for them, get their panties in a bunch—

The laugh caught in her throat, and she began to choke. No, not choke. Choking required something to be lodged in your throat. She simply couldn't breathe, as though her lungs were incapable of absorbing oxygen.

The sudden lack of airflow caused her heartbeat to accelerate, and she leaned against the nearest wall for support, almost falling against it.

Asima's air of annoyance dropped and was replaced with concern. She rushed to Gram' elbow and gripped it, helping her up.

"Mother," she said, using a word that Gram didn't know but recognized as a title of respect, "Are you all right?"

Gram realized that she was able to breathe again. The intake of air was easier than what she'd become used to over the past few months, but it wasn't as easy to breathe as it had been just moments before. The genie's magic was wearing off.

She righted herself, suddenly lightheaded as she instinctively breathed in quickly and deeply, compensating for the moments when she'd been without oxygen.

"I'm fine. I... I guess I'm not used to the heat."

"I'll get you some water," Asima said after forcefully guiding Gram to a chair. She seemed afraid that she'd falter again—Gram suddenly realized that if she collapsed here, that would be it. There was no ambulance to call, no emergency oxygen tanks hidden away in some back room. She would die.

Thaddeus had told her to get back to the library as soon as she felt the magic weaken. Well, that must have been it, though she hadn't expected it to come so suddenly. She remembered the way back to the gate well enough—she'd made sure to note intersections and other landmarks in her mind's eye as she walked down the streets. She could make it back there no problem, she was certain.

But then what would happen to April and Dorian? How would they get home?

The decision was easy, almost as if there was no decision to make at all. She'd lived a long life; if anyone should be at risk, it should be her. But she had to hurry.

The madam came back with a clay cup of water. Gram ignored it. She didn't have time.

"Where is my granddaughter?"

Asima raised an eyebrow. "I can see where your granddaughter gets her attitude," she remarked.

"Please—I don't have much time. If you know where they are, tell me."

Asima sighed. "Drink the water and I'll tell you."

Gram took the small cup, and lifted it to her lips. The water tasted earthy—that must be from the cup—but also sweet, without chemicals. It had never been filtered through a machine.

She drained the cup, not realizing how thirsty she'd been. She didn't protest when Asima refilled it. She needed to be hydrated if she was going to make it to April.

Once she'd emptied the second cup, Asima sighed. "I don't know where your granddaughter is—but I know where they were, and where the djinni is now."

"Where?" Gram asked.

"Word got back to me as soon as it happened. They encountered a man whom witnesses described as deformed. This deformed man confronted them."

"Deformed?" That could mean any number of things.

Asima shrugged. "Some say his skin was black, as though he'd recently been badly burned. Most say that he kept himself covered. He was also immensely tall."

That sounded like Hank Rottman. The thought of his name reminded Gram that he was alone with Thaddeus at that very moment. Her heart fluttered. Being alone with this man put Thaddeus in danger.

"And?" Gram asked, prompting her to continue.

"You are familiar with the bonds of the djinn, are you not?"

Gram nodded, but she must not have looked very convincing because Asima explained anyway.

"The djinn are powerful creatures. Allah created them when he created men. Men were molded from the clay of the earth, but the djinn were crafted from fire. Very powerful, but with one weakness: they can be bound to physical objects. The red djinni, the owner of this establishment, is bound to one such object, a ring."

"You don't say?" Gram said, pushing her hand deeper into her pocket. She'd been trying to keep the ink rot out of sight so as not to alarm anyone, but now she had reason to keep the ring hidden as well. It would be a prize for anyone who wanted it, so it was best that she not advertise that she had it—especially because she wasn't sure if she'd be able to fend off anyone who decided they wanted it.

"Yes. The ring is very precious. Somehow it fell into the wrong hands."

"The deformed man," Gram clarified. "Can you tell me anything else?"

Asima nodded. "He confronted the djinni and your granddaughter as they were making their way towards your little doorway."

"You know about the door?" That seemed like something they'd want to keep secret.

"Of course. It is my job to know what is going on in the walls of this establishment—that means the origins and intent of anyone who enters it."

Gram nodded. That made sense. "So what happened next?" She'd seen what happened with her own eyes, but maybe Asima would have some new information, some context or perspective that she lacked.

"The deformed man commanded the djinni to destroy the building containing your door. He now guards it to make sure that your granddaughter and her companion don't approach. My sources say that they ran off. I don't know what became of them."

Gram placed the cup down on the ledge. If she could get to the genie she could use the ring to command him to stop. Hopefully he'd be able to fix the damage to the door, like Thaddeus said.

"How do I get to the door from here?"

Asima's expression grew concerned. "You cannot possibly be thinking of going there," she said. "I've received word that he's not letting *anyone* near that building."

"I'll be fine," Gram said. Inside her pocket she worried the ring with her thumb. She had it, so she'd be able to stop him from causing any more damage. But she had to get there first. Every breath was more difficult than the last. She had thirty minutes, forty-five at most, to get to the genie.

Asima noticed her worry. "You don't seem like you believe that yourself."

"I have to try," Gram said, resolute.

"There is no way I can talk you out of this, Mother?"

Gram shook her head.

Asima sighed. "Then I will send one of the girls with you, in case you succumb to the heat again." She looked over her shoulder and called out. "Rhea!"

A few moments later Rhea walked back from the front of the building. "Yes, madam?"

"Take this woman to the djinni. You know where he is?"

Rhea nodded her head. "The men out front were talking about it. They think he's lost his mind."

Gram wondered if the citizens of this city knew that the genie was, in fact, a magical being. It seemed like the women and men who worked in the House of Fire knew it, but did he advertise that fact to the outside world?

Her eyes fell on Rhea. She couldn't endanger this girl. "Thanks for the offer, but it's best you stay here. Directions will be sufficient."

"Are you sure, Mother? Pardon my frankness, but you look to be at death's threshold, yourself."

"Than that makes me the best candidate for the job. I won't lead anyone there with me."

Asima considered this, then nodded.

Rhea's face contorted in a look of worry. "Will the djinni come back? What will happen to us if he doesn't?"

"Pray that he comes back," Asima said, "then pray that if he doesn't, whoever owns this place next is as generous as he is."

Gram balked. If she'd been in the Asima's shoes, she would have reassured the girl that the genie would come back, rather than make her fearful that he wouldn't. Rhea was still young, even if this world considered her a woman.

Rhea's eyes widened at Asima's words, but she thrust her chin upwards defiantly, her full lips pressed into a thin line, and told Gram the directions to the courtyard.

Gram nodded. She needed to get to the genie before she ran out of time.

Chapter 8

The desert air burned April's lungs as she and Dorian ran across the city. Merchants chanted at them as they passed, trying to entice them to buy rugs or pans or chickens. Her breathing was sharp and painful, but in a familiar way she felt that she could withstand. She wasn't sure if it was the workout Randall led her through before every training session or the gate's influence, but she was in the best shape she'd ever been in.

Dorian lagged behind her by five, then ten, and soon twenty paces. Apparently he didn't get as much exercise as she did. Made sense—aerobics classes didn't exist in nineteenth-century England.

She lessened her pace until she was jogging beside him. She expected him to protest, but he didn't. He clutched one hand to his side, nursing a stitch.

"Maybe you should take up exercising," she said mildly.

"Like I have the time or opportunity," Dorian said. "I'm busy the entire night when I'm in your world, and my servants think I'm crazy enough as it is. They don't need to see me doing crunches. They'd think I was possessed by the devil."

"I mean, I just think you'd be healthier."

He snorted. "I've lived well over seventy years. You need not worry about my longevity." He was quiet for a few moments as his breathing returned to normal. "I bet your genie works out," he muttered sullenly.

"Probably," April mused. She doubted that he *needed* to do any physical exercise to get the six-pack that he was so proud of flaunting. He was made of flame, after all, and could probably choose his human form. But showing off by doing pull-ups and push-ups was just the sort of thing he'd do.

She didn't realize she was smiling until Dorian said, "Calm down before you start drooling."

Her face colored. He thought her expression had come from lust rather than amusement.

"It's not like that," she said. "I thought it was funny. The genie showing off by exercising when he probably doesn't even *need* to, you know? He's such a show boat."

Dorian was quiet for a moment, and she realized that their pace had slowed down to a brusque walk.

"So what's the deal, then?" he asked quietly. "You and the genie?"

"I don't know," she said honestly. She'd been dealing with the same question ever since they stepped foot in this world.

They walked for several seconds in silence.

"I don't expect you to spare my feelings," Dorian said finally. "But it would be nice if you didn't flaunt it in front of me."

A feeling that she couldn't quite place her finger on erupted in her chest. Was it anger or fear, or a mix of the two? All she knew for sure was that it was intense and she wished she wasn't feeling it. Things would be so much easier for both of them if she wasn't.

Anger was the simplest and easiest possibility to deal with. "Listen, I can't help the way you feel," she said. "And I don't want to cause you any discomfort or pain, and I *definitely* don't want things to be awkward between us. You have to understand that I didn't want any of this to happen. This is all the genie's doing. And I was involved with the genie before you even told me how you felt. It's not like I started sleeping with him out of spite or anything."

"It's not like things between us would be any different if you weren't sleeping with the genie," Dorian said accusatorily.

April stopped walking. He was speaking like she'd rejected him. "*You're* the one who nipped any possibility of an *us*"—she waved her hand back and forth between him to make sure he knew what she meant—"not me, remember? You never gave me a chance to say how I felt."

Dorian's face had started out angry, ready to lash out for whatever she'd said. But his eyes widened, and his mouth opened to form an o.

She winced, realizing what she'd said. *Why* had she said it? Why did she insist on making things more awkward between them? He'd already made it clear that a relationship between them would never work out.

She braced herself for him to ask how she did feel. She'd stupidly opened up the floor for him to do so, even though she didn't have a straight answer.

He paused for a moment. He breathed in, opening his mouth slightly as though getting ready to speak, but then he closed it again and shook his head. "This... this is a conversation for another time, I think," he said. "Right now we have someplace to be."

It was her turn for her eyes to widen. Somehow, as much as she'd been dreading having to explain her own hard-to-discern feelings, this lack of catharsis was worse.

Still, she nodded. "You're right." She turned back in the direction of the door. "Let's pick up the pace."

Dorian groaned like a kid in gym class being hounded by the P.E. teacher, but started to move quickly again.

Chapter 9

"These bonds are entirely unnecessary," Rottman said. "I won't run away or try to overpower you."

"There's not a snowflake's chance in hell of me removing them," Thaddeus said.

"We both know you could recast this enchantment in a heartbeat, before I could take three steps. I just don't see why you should tire yourself."

"Gee, thanks for your concern," Thaddeus said sarcastically, "but I'm fine." It was true. This bond spell, which restrained a person to a physical spot like a pair of handcuffs, was only mildly taxing. "Nice try."

Rottman shrugged. "Suit yourself. I'm only thinking of your comfort."

Thaddeus looked at Rottman. Rottman looked back at him. He couldn't deny it any longer—the man's skin had taken on a pale flesh tone. At some angles, parts of his body still looked like viscous purple-black ink, but for the most part his skin was the light peachy nude color of a Caucasian skin that didn't get enough sun. It was a shade very close to Thaddeus' own pale flesh.

Rottman was starting to look more and more human, like a cheap CGI rendering. There was still something unreal about him, some uncanniness that the monster wasn't yet able to overcome, but Thaddeus was certain that he'd soon look just as lifelike and human as anyone walking the streets of Minneapolis.

This scared Thaddeus more than anything he'd seen so far, either during his short time working with the Pagewalker or all his years at the Agency.

"How are you doing that?" Thaddeus asked.

Rottman looked down at his own flesh-colored hand. The knuckles and joints were still black, as though he'd been working on a car all day an engine grease had gotten pressed into the crags there.

Rottman looked up at Thaddeus and smiled. "Do you remember when you dropped that vial of serum on the ground in Jekyll's lab?"

Thaddeus nodded. "I don't see what that has to do with my question."

"We'll get to that." A smile bloomed on Rottman's face. His teeth were beginning to take on the off-white hue of normal teeth, but the lines between and behind them were punctuated by that black color, giving him the look of someone who has spent their entire life gorging on candy and sugar without intervention from a dentist.

Rottman continued. "Before that, I saw into every world where I was present, witnessing, but never having the faculties to interpret or judge what I saw. Then that tiny splash of liquid fell onto the *tiniest* arm of one of my spores. And everything changed. I suppose I have you to thank for all this."

Thaddeus was uncomfortable with this assessment. "Officer Powers was the one who ingested the serum while you were attached to him." Thaddeus was about to tell him not to hold this over his head as though it were his fault, but he stopped himself. He didn't want Rottman to know how much his words bothered him.

The words of his commander at the Academy echoed in his ears: *Never let them see you flinch.*

"True," Rottman conceded. "I would have been introduced to the serum no matter what—of course, the fact that Powers found the serum at all was, in fact, a direct result of your reckless actions." He paused. "The first, unadulterated drop, though." He sighed contentedly as though remembering something very pleasurable. "It sped things up. When Officer Powers took the serum, I would have experienced everything secondhand. There's no way to know for sure, but I believe I wouldn't be this advanced right now if I hadn't had that first drop. I'd get here eventually, maybe months or years down the road. Who knows—perhaps you and the Pagewalker would have discovered my existence and destroyed me before I was able to do much."

Thaddeus took in all this information in stride. "Are you trying to chip away at my resolve?" he said. "Make the magic bonds binding you weaker? Because it won't work."

Rottman didn't even test the magical cords binding his wrists. "I have no doubt that your resolve—and your magic—are strong. I know that from the last time that we went head to head."

Thaddeus thought of the minutes he'd spent in Jekyll's doorway holding William the Brutal, whom Rottman had apparently been attached to at the time, at bay while he waited for April to come back from the library with a syringe so they could administer the serum that would reverse the effects of Jekyll's potion. It had been excruciating to maintain the concentration, and William the Brutal had been a formidable opponent. He knew now that the

fact that the ink rot had been attached to him had fortified the malformed police officer.

Thaddeus shrugged. "Anyone would have been able to do it," he said. "It was
what was necessary."

"Not true." Rottman shook his head. "Give yourself some credit."

"I don't need your approval, thanks." He didn't like this string of thinking.
How had they gotten on this subject, anyway? He'd been asking Rottman why
his skin was changing color.

A flame of embarrassment entered his chest as he realized that Rottman
had been distracting him away from that question. That meant it was important.

"What does that have to do with your skin changing color?" Thaddeus
asked.

"It relates, I promise," Rottman said. "As I was saying, before touching
Jekyll's serum I witnessed everything that was going on around me, but didn't
have any way to process that information. Jekyll's serum taught me how to
change—and evolve."

"You're becoming more and more human."

Rottman swiveled his head and squinted as though testing Thaddeus' assessment in his mind's eye. "Kind of, though I am still the rot you've come to
know and love." He smiled at his own joke. "Just a whole lot smarter, and now
able to change at will. You see, the serum was designed to affect the human
body. Humans, as impressive as you are, are not very malleable. Your bodies can
renew themselves, but they can't deviate much from the blueprints they were
born with."

"How do you know all that? About the human body renewing itself, I
mean." Thaddeus asked. Rottman seemed like he wanted to talk. This was a
good opportunity to acquire some intel. He just hoped that Rottman's loose
lips were a symptom of naiveté rather than from knowing something Thaddeus
didn't.

"Like I said—I witnessed everything from everywhere I've been. You know
as well as I do that there are medical texts in the Werner collection, as well
as texts within the story worlds themselves. They might be a little outdated
compared to the knowledge this world has amassed in the last sixty years, but
they're a start."

"So you just *know* everything that you've ever seen in any of these books?" This information made Thaddeus uneasy. That was *a lot* of information.

"Heavens, no." Rottman chuckled. "It's *available* to me, but I still have to go and make the effort to read the books and study the information, or listen to any of the conversations I've overheard. It's like a mental experiment, I'd say. It takes effort, and my memory is as faulty as yours. There's also the problem of the information I've gathered being wildly inconsistent. I suppose human knowledge has changed over the centuries that these books span."

Thaddeus considered this. This was still troubling, but better than Rottman having instant access to all the information he could possibly want.

Thaddeus turned to the other thing that Rottman had said that bothered him. "You said that humans can't change themselves. You can?"

Rottman showed his nasty teeth again. "You know I can rearrange myself. Build myself up, disassemble and rearrange. You've seen it."

Thaddeus remembered the ink monster unravelling top to bottom, like a reverse 3D-printer. He'd watched the snake-like strands of rot slither across the brick road and reassemble themselves at a different point down the street.

"So?" Thaddeus asked.

"As I grew and learned and became more advanced, I began to wonder if I could do the same on a microscopic level. As you saw when I first arrived, I succeeded to a certain degree at replicating a human person."

"Barely," Thaddeus said. "Your craftsmanship needs work." He didn't point out that Rottman now looked more human, though he hadn't lost that uncanny aspect yet. There was still something off about him.

"You're right," Rottman conceded. "No matter how much I tried to replicate those around me, I just couldn't perfect it. Especially the colors." He sighed. "Then I realized—I was copying a copy, wasn't I? Books offer a secondhand perspective at best. Some information was bound to get lost in the process. I needed to study the real thing. Unfortunately, even with all the information I had at my fingertips, I never had access to that."

"What are you talking about?" Thaddeus said. He really didn't like the way this conversation was going, and judging by the pained burning in the back of his mind, neither did the gate.

"The worlds of these books are beautifully rendered, aren't they? By all estimations, they are real, right down to the thoughts and emotions felt by their

inhabitants. But they are still created, and therefore lack any real ability to create themselves. Tell me—do you think if you perused the book shelves of any of
these worlds, that the literature available there would differ from what is available here? Beyond what is outlined in the texts that describe them, of course."

"I don't know," Thaddeus said. He'd never thought about it.

"I'll tell you the answer—it's no. Your world is a creative one. So creative,
that from it sprang universes so well thought-out that they were able to become
real. How miraculous is that? So I thought, if I wanted to achieve my goal of
becoming human, I needed to come here, learn from *this* world."

"Becoming human?" Thaddeus said.

Rottman nodded. "Seeming human, I suppose. No matter how good a
mimic I become, I can't change what I am."

"Mimic?" Thaddeus said.

Rottman smiled, and before his eyes, his features began to shift. Thaddeus
stood and stepped back, the chair he'd been sitting on falling over in the
process. He almost lost his hold on the spell binding Rottman's wrists, but he
remembered at the last second and held on.

He watched in horror as Rottman's forehead became broader and his skin
darkened, until the ebony eyes looking back at him did so from Randall's face.

The effect wasn't perfect; there remained that last bit of uncanniness that
betrayed his inhumanness. If the real Randall and this facsimile were placed
side-by-side, you'd be able to easily tell this one was fake.

Rottman's features shifted again, becoming smaller and more delicate, the
skin lightening to a peachy alabaster, until it was April's face that stared back at
him. She smiled, but her teeth were black and rotten.

Then Rottman shifted again until the face staring back at him was familiar,
but not as familiar as the others. It was a face Thaddeus had known his entire
life, but only occasionally saw when he was looking at a photograph or a mir-
ror—his own.

Compared to the others, it looked the most realistic. Why wouldn't it?
Rottman had over an hour of quality alone-time to get every feature exactly
right.

"We will destroy you," Thaddeus said, unable to keep the revulsion from his
voice.

His own face smiled back at him with blackened teeth.

Chapter 10

The air seemed to grow heavier as April and Dorian approached the gate. What if their plan didn't work? There was so much that could go wrong. Maybe there was no djinni in this ring. Maybe her genie would easily overpower him.

An even worse thought occurred to her: what if this ring's djinni was stronger than her genie? What if he was killed? What if she had to order him to be killed?

The smell of cooking kabobs wafted around the next corner. The scent of meat turned her nervous stomach lurch, and she fought the nausea roiling at the back of her throat. She didn't remember a food vendor on this street when they'd walked through it earlier.

A boy wearing a loose linen vest ran past them, his shoulder colliding with her hip.

"Ow." She massaged the assaulted bone, but the boy didn't stop.

"Cool water and clean cloths!" the boy called ahead of him, to whom April didn't know. He receded into the distance.

That wasn't a good sign. She met Dorian's eye, and he nodded. They hurried around the corner. A throng of people gathered twenty paces away. A dozen men stood, talking to each other tensely, while an equal number of women knelt in throngs of three or four. The men gestured wildly down the street in the direction of the gate.

"What do you think they're so upset about?" Dorian said wryly, his tone suggesting that he knew exactly what was upsetting them.

April didn't answer. She was more interested in the women kneeling in groups on the ground. They spoke rapidly amongst themselves, the older women issuing commands to their younger counterparts. April approached one group, trying to see what they worked so feverishly on.

One woman lifted a knife, deftly slicing at something April couldn't see. She put the knife carefully on the ground beside her, and then began to pull. April moved closer to see what was in her hand—a length a fabric that at one time had been the leg of a pair of pants. It was singed and covered in black char. The woman rose and moved away, taking the knife as she did, supposedly to dispose of the pants elsewhere. This offered a view of the man she'd been attending to. He looked to be in his late twenties. Burns covered the right side of his body up to his neck. There was no blood; the fire had cauterized the wounds instantly.

It wasn't kabobs that April had been smelling. She turned to the side, and her stomach surrendered its contents. She felt Dorian's cool hands pull her ponytail, which had long since become loose and unruly, back away from her face.

"He'll survive," a voice behind them said, "if the fever from the wounds doesn't take him."

April stood. The voice came from a middle-aged man, probably in his late forties. Like most of the men she'd seen he wore a loose, light-colored tunic and pants.

"What happened here?" Dorian asked.

"The abandoned dwelling at the end of the street collapsed. We were heading to the building to check for survivors. When we reached the edge of that building"—he pointed to a single-story structure about halfway between where they were standing and the remains of the gate—"*he* blasted us with fire. Then after we retreated, he had the gall to call to us and tell us the building had been empty. As though we could trust anything that he says."

April turned towards the genie, who stood in front of the demolished building, about sixty feet away. He met her gaze. Even at this distance his eyes were like two coals burning in his face. She'd never seen such power emanating from him.

"If the building was abandoned, why would anyone be inside?"

"Homeless people congregate in abandoned buildings. Children even use them to play while avoiding chores. Pray to Allah that neither is the case."

She thought back to all the times that she'd entered and exited the gate that day. Had she seen anyone? Not that she remembered, but that didn't mean no one was there. She fought the urge to vomit again.

She wanted to believe that the genie wasn't capable of this carnage, but she'd known in her heart that he was the cause from the second she saw the burned man, even from when she'd first smelled burning flesh. It didn't matter that the genie hadn't done it of his own free will: he was powerful, and dangerous.

"We have to get up there," she said to Dorian. "We have to stop him."

She started to move in the genie's direction again, but the man stepped in her path. "It is unwise to get closer, sister."

"We'll be fine," April said, even though she wasn't sure that it was the truth. They were probably in more danger than anyone. They were the ones the genie was tasked to keep away from the gate, after all.

The man waved his arm at them as though shooing a bee, absolving himself of any culpability for their fate. "When you feel the heat of a hundred suns on your skin, remember that I warned you." He turned and headed to warn another group of people who were walking up to see what the commotion was about.

"Ready?" she asked Dorian, and he nodded.

They walked towards the genie. As they approached, his stance became tighter, more offensive. When they reached the edge of the building, he raised one hand.

"Stay back," he said. "I won't have any choice but to hurt you."

"And you know that we don't have any choice, either," April called out to him. "We need to stop Rottman."

He narrowed his eyes. April wouldn't have been able to tell from this distance if they weren't glowing so brightly in the first place.

"Have you seen those men behind you? Some barely escaped with their lives. They will carry scars as long as they live. Don't make me hurt you, as well." The last words were choked.

"What can I do?" she asked. "If I stay here we all die—or Rottman comes back. Whatever he has planned won't be good for any of us. If we can get through the gate I can get your ring back. I can set you free."

The genie laughed, a harsh sound. "To get through that gate you will have to kill me first. It makes my freedom a moot point, don't you think?" his gaze darkened. "Do it, if you get the chance. The long sleep is preferable to a life of slavery."

April's heart quickened. Killing the genie was a possibility, of course. She'd known this the whole time, but hadn't let herself think about it. As much as she was hurt by the genie's manipulations, she didn't want to hurt him, let alone kill him. But she didn't see any way of getting past him without bloodshed.

"We can distract you," she called, "and slip by then."

The genie laughed again. "Sorceress," he used his pet name for her almost mournfully, "I gave you the nickname of a powerful magic wielder, but we both know that any power you have comes from the broken doorway behind me. You're no match for me. It's suicide to try."

"You're right," she said, "I can't do anything myself. However..."

She reached into her pocket and pulled out the sapphire ring. She lifted it aloft in the palm of her hand so that the sun glinted off of it.

The genie squinted again, then his eyes widened. The effect was similar to a coals in a fire suddenly rising in intensity. Then he smiled. "Clever girl."

She started to slip the ring on her finger, but then hesitated. "This genie might have to kill you," she said, her voice small. Could she deal with that? She wouldn't be dealing the death blow herself, but it would be coming from her orders.

The genie thought about this for a moment, then he nodded. "Then so be it," he said. Then he grinned. "But they have to best me, first."

She nodded, and after another moment's hesitation, slipped the ring on her finger.

Nothing happened.

She panicked for a moment. She'd thought the genie would simply appear. Had she grabbed a ring that no longer had a genie attached to it? She knew it was possible, since her genie's ring was vacant after she'd freed him...

"What's wrong?" Her voice cracked.

"The ring is dormant. You need to summon them," the genie called to her. He sounded worried.

"Is that a bad thing?" she called.

"It's not a good thing," the genie replied. "The magician liked to keep those he subjugated around. It gave him a power kick to be able to flaunt them in front of each other and others. So if he didn't let this one out, there was a reason."

"Like what?"

"Maybe they were especially volatile and would take whatever action they were able to thwart the magician."

"That means they're likely to turn on us, too," Dorian said.

The genie nodded, a rare moment of agreement between him and Dorian. "Bargain with them. Tell them if they cooperate you will free them. It creates a binding contract between you." he paused, then added, "If you plan to limit their magic after their freedom as you did mine, for the love of Allah, don't tell them beforehand."

"But they have to do as I say, right? Do I really need a contract?" It seemed like a lot of extra work, and could take time they didn't have.

"What you say, and what you say *only*," the genie responded. "If they can find a different meaning for your words, they will. Let's just say it's better to have them on your side."

April remembered how the cobalt genie had been able to let them into the magician's house because of the technicality that they weren't local. She needed to be careful with how she worded her commands. "How do I summon them?"

"Worry the ring's stone with your fingers," the genie said.

She did, silently kicking herself. How had she forgotten that she had to rub the ring? Any kid who'd ever watched a Disney movie knew that.

"Now you have to call them forth verbally," the genie directed.

She nodded, but when she opened her mouth to speak, the genie interrupted her. "Remember, my life is not the only one in danger here. They may end up killing me, or I may end up killing them. I have to do whatever is necessary to protect this building. Just know that if it comes to that... I didn't mean it."

April nodded. "I know." She rubbed the ring again. "I call forth the genie of this sapphire ring."

The ring grew hot beneath her fingers. A stream of smoke began to emanate from beneath her fingers, thin and winding like from an incense stick. It grew thicker and darkened, and began to gather into an opaque cloud in front of her.

The cloud became so dense that she couldn't see through it. After a few seconds it dissipated, revealing a short humanoid form in front of her. As the smoke thinned out, April looked into two large, brown eyes. They were set into an equally round cherubic face. A long, black braid was slung over a shoulder.

April gazed into the defiant eyes of a girl no more than ten years old.

~~~

Gram's feet weren't quite doing what she told them to do any more. It was a familiar feeling, one she'd grown accustomed to over the previous few years. It was amazing that it felt so strange to her now. Just a couple hours of false strength had spoiled her.

Her breath, too, came with difficulty. It burned in her chest, but also seemed to not do anything, her lungs unable to absorb oxygen quickly enough. Static ringed the edges of her vision. It had been there for a good ten minutes, but now it jumped inwards sporadically as her body threatened to give way under all the strain.

She wanted nothing more than to stop and catch her breath, but rest wouldn't replenish her stamina the way it had in her younger days. If she sat down now, she'd never rise again.

And the genie's touch hadn't completely worn off yet. Things were only going to get worse. To stop now would be to waste the little of magical strength that remained.

A long, smooth stick lay on the ground in front of her. She leaned down to grab it. The static almost meeting in the middle of her field of vision, but she managed to grasp onto a six-inch nub protruding from the side of the stick and pick it up. She stood, leaning on the stick. For several scary moments it was the only thing keeping her upright.

She allowed herself a few seconds' reprieve. Then she looked to the edge of the next building. There appeared to be space beyond it. Was that the turn that Asima had mentioned?

She focused on pulling herself forward towards the edge of the building, step by step.

She thought back to when she first got serious about exercising. April would never believe it—this thought made Gram smile in spite of her situation—but she hadn't always been in as good of shape as April remembered her. She'd always been thin thanks to a fast metabolism, but her body had been no muscle and all fat.

When she'd started gaining weight in her fifties, she reluctantly started going to the gym. It had been so hard in those first few months to push past the stitches that gripped her sides and the dull ache in her legs as she ran on the treadmill. That discomfort had never really gone away; it was always there when she worked out. She'd just learned to push through it.

That's all she had to do now. Push past the pain.

She hobbled forward, mere steps away from the edge of the building... if she'd had any breath to spare, she would have held it in anticipation of finding a narrow alley...

But it was just a small yard; the space ended in a dead end where another larger house lay behind the one she'd passed.

Bitter disappointment filled her. She nearly collapsed, again leaning on her walking stick for support. She felt tears prick at the corners of her eyes. For a moment defeat washed over her; there was no way she could move on. She'd failed April.

April.

She looked up to see a passerby, a young man, slow as he passed her, his face scrunching into a look of concern.

"Mother, are you all right?" he asked. "Do you live nearby? I could have one of your sons come get you."

"The collapsed house," she said, having to pause to take wheezing breathes. "Where is it?" she asked. Asima had said word had spread about the house's fall; she hoped this young man would have heard of it.

He pointed up the street, though she couldn't pinpoint the exact spot he was looking at. "Just down the next alley," he said. "But you must not go there. There is a crazed djinn who burns anyone who draws too close. Even if you were well, it would not be safe for you."

"My granddaughter," she paused to breathe, "Is in danger."

The boy's eyes widened. "You do not mean that house is yours?" he asked. "I regret to tell you it is completely destroyed. I saw it myself before I thought better of being there and left. No one could have survived that. I am sorry." His eyes widened as they fell on her ink rot-covered hand. "What happened to you? You must see a healer immediately."

She was unable to respond, even in a one-word answer. She didn't even try. She needed to use her remaining strength to get to April.

She pressed forward in the direction he'd pointed. She focused on what she thought was the farthest point he could have meant. *I only have to go that far, then I can turn,* she thought. *That's not so far. I can do it. For April.*

The young man followed her for several paces, then he seemed to give up. Before he left, he said, "May Allah be with you. I hope that your granddaughter is safe."

Me, too, she thought. But she had faith in April. She'd lived through so much.

She pressed on, ignoring the bitter disappointment as she passed each house that might have an alley next to it—none of them did.

She started picking things that were close by, five feet away or less, and thinking, *I only have to walk to that cart,* or, *that door.* As soon as she passed each one, she focused on something else.

She passed another house. She'd already given up hope that it would be next to the alley that she needed...

But instead of the dark presence of another building, she could see an imperfect line of light between buildings—the alley. Relief washed over her, but she ignored it. She had no time to celebrate.

A figure stood about a hundred yards away. Luckily her eyes were one of the few parts of her body that still worked as they were supposed to. Even with the black static eating at the edge of her vision, she recognized the genie's billowing, brightly-colored clothes as well as his proud, straight posture.

Tears prickled at the corners of her eyes, but she blinked them away. The genie was still so very far away. In her youth she might have traversed this distance within a minute or two, but now it would take a marathon's worth of energy.

Maybe she could call to him, give her command from this far away? Thaddeus had said that he only needed to hear her and see her.

She opened her mouth, but even with all of her energy being forced into them, the sound she was able to produce was barely more than a whisper. The sound was too quiet; there was no way he'd hear her.

At that moment the last of the genie's touch left her body. She doubled over, feeling worse than she had before he'd touched her. Maybe she'd been using borrowed energy, or maybe she was feeling the exhaustion from having pushed herself so far. Maybe she'd just gotten used to feeling normal again.

It didn't matter. How could she keep going? Still doubled over, she used the walking stick to pull herself forward. The effort was enough to throw her into a wheezing fit. She waited for the fit to pass, then took another step.

She managed to take ten steps in as many minutes. She looked forward to where the alley widened, a distance of about thirty feet. The genie was talking to someone she couldn't see.

She squinted at the side of the building on the side of the alley opposite where the genie was standing. The building was shorter than all the rest, and made out of discernable bricks rather than solid adobe or stone. There was movement there, but she couldn't quite make it out...

Then the person stepped forward half a foot, and April's face came into view, only visible from the side, and only to a point just behind her cheekbones. But it was undoubtedly her granddaughter.

"April," Gram wheezed. Seeing April's face replenished her energy slightly, and she was able to make the next dozen steps in what felt like half the time... but soon she was wheezing again.

Despair filled her as she saw the distance between her and the place where she needed to be. She found herself hoping that they'd see her, then they could come to her... but what reason would they have to look down this dark alley? They didn't even know she was coming.

As though she'd been punched in the gut, she collapsed down onto her knees, and began to crawl, still clutching the walking stick.

She could no longer tell how far she'd gone, and she didn't look behind her to check.

She allowed her cheek to come to a rest in the dirt. She was surprised by how little she had to lower herself down to do so. She was going to die here. She found that preferable to living with the knowledge that she'd doomed April.

A loud braying sound from her left forced her eyes open. Without moving even her head, she directed her eyes toward the source of the noise—a donkey tied to a short wooden stake next to the nearest building. It faced the direction she'd been heading in, but looked at her sidelong with mild interest.

Painfully, she pulled herself to her feet. Her vision blacked out. She leaned against the stick it returned—what was left of it, anyway; it now seemed like she was looking out at the world from the inside of a tunnel, the blackness taking up at least half of her sight. A distant thought entered her mind: She'd passed out. She had no idea how she'd managed to stay upright.

When she was fairly sure she wasn't going to pass out again, she hobbled the two steps to the donkey. With a shaking hand, she unhooked the rope that tied him to the stake. There was no saddle or stirrups to help her onto the beast's back; she had no idea how she would mount it. In the end she settled for simply leaning over it, more a fall than a deliberate, controlled motion, the upper half of her body on one side of the donkey and her legs on the other. It was uncomfortable, but she wouldn't be conscious for much longer to experience that discomfort. And the position seemed stable enough that she wouldn't fall to the earth as the donkey moved, which was all she could hope for.

As the tunnel in her vision grew longer and darker, almost as though the outside world was speeding further and further away, she used her last bit of strength to poke the donkey's hindquarters with the stick.

With a bray of protest, the donkey lurched forward. The back and forth motion was almost soothing as the world receded into a pinprick of light, then disappeared entirely.

~~~

"You took a *child?*" The genie called at her, disgust in his voice. "I take back my comment about you being clever."

"It was the only ring left!" April called back, panic filling her voice. "How was I supposed to know!" She'd really messed up. How could she send this little girl to fight the genie?

The genie spoke several words in a language that she didn't understand, but she could tell that he was cursing. He switched back to English. "How am I supposed to fight a child? A *girl?*"

The girl turned towards the genie. Her eyes flashed in that familiar-but-terrifying way.

"My mother was a high priestess of the Ifrit, my father a trusted advisor of the King of Sand!" she said proudly. "All my life I've had to deal with men thinking they're better than me, thinking they can own me. You are as foolish as they are."

The genie raised his eyebrows at the girl's words. "Be that as it may, child, you are outmatched not by power or heritage, but by experience." The gentleness seeming out of place in his voice.

"We shall see." The girl turned back to April. "You are the one who freed the djinni of the red ring, are you not?"

April nodded. "I am. How did you know?"

"I heard you speaking while I was in the ring."

"You can hear from inside there?" Dorian asked.

The girl didn't look at him as she answered, her eyes never leaving April. "Sometimes."

"I accept your offer of freedom in exchange for helping you reach that building safely," the girl said. "Even if you choose to place a caveat on the bonds as you did for the djinni of the red ring."

April thought for a moment. "These are bold words, and I can tell you mean every syllable. You are obviously a very smart, very capable girl. But I can't ask you to do this. You're too young."

The girl lifted her chin defiantly. "I am older than you are by hundreds of years."

The genie, who seemed able to hear their conversation, responded. "It's true," he said. "Our life spans exceed those of humans. But she is immature still."

The girl ignored the genie. Her eyes blazed. "I can show you, Mistress. Will you allow me to demonstrate my power?"

April thought for only a moment before nodding. "Okay," she said. "But no one gets hurt, you understand? No tricks." If it came from her mouth, it was a command, and the girl had to obey it.

The girl nodded. Her expression did not hint at whether she'd planned any tricks or not.

She turned away, walking back in the direction of the crowd who waited behind them. Many of the people there started to move backwards from the girl. The voices of the crowd grew louder as everyone jockeyed to vacate the street.

The girl waited for the injured to be carried away. As she did, Dorian leaned into April and whispered, "Are you sure this is a good idea?"

"I told her no tricks," April said.

"Something tells me that's not specific enough," Dorian said.

April didn't respond. The girl seemed honest and forthright. She hoped the hunch was correct.

The girl watched as the last of the people moved away. Those that had remained to watch what happened now stood another thirty feet behind where they'd been originally.

Satisfied that they were at a safe distance, the girl lifted each of her hands, stretching her arms away from herself. Heat lines began to waver in the air, extending out from her arms in curving lines. *Not heat*, April thought. *Magic*.

Once the distortion from the heat magic grew so strong that everything behind them became smudged and distorted, the girl let out a guttural cry. It was a sound not of distress, but of power.

Then she brought her hands together in one swift move, like she'd caught a mosquito between them right in front of her face. The buildings before her groaned, a sound like a bulldozer moving earth, but without the beeping and mechanical whirring. Clouds of sand and dust erupted into the air. It was as though they were witnessing an earthquake.

The girl lowered her arms, her body still tense, surveying the results of her efforts. The distortion in the air dissipated quickly; the dust took longer to disperse. When it did, April gasped.

The road was gone—the houses lining each side of the street now curved together to meet in the middle, blocking the path and the onlookers who had been there moments before. Terrified voices cried on the other sides of the building, though no one seemed to be calling out in pain, only fright. The voices quickly receded. April saw faces pressed against the lattice windows of some of the buildings that had been moved, but they moved away quickly, hopefully to exit on the far side of the building.

It seemed the girl had kept her word about not harming anyone.

She turned back, a satisfied smile on her face. She seemed to wait for April's reaction. The display was impressive, but was it enough to match the genie?

She turned back to him. His mouth was open, his face expanded in surprise. He quickly closed his jaw when he saw her looking at him.

"The girl possesses power," he conceded reluctantly. "But not enough to ensure she would beat me out of hand." He seemed to say this mostly as a warning—but April detected a little bit of jealousy in his voice. Even now he was worried about his reputation. Typical.

She waved the girl back. She didn't appear remotely tired. She smiled smugly.

"The magician thinks my magic skills are undeveloped because of my age, just as I wanted him to," she said. "If he knew I could do these things, he would never have left me dormant."

April looked at Dorian. Were they really going to send in a kid to fight the genie? *A djinn kid who can reorder giant buildings without destroying them,* she reminded herself. The girl was more than she appeared to be.

She needed to talk to the girl, but the genie had made it clear that he could hear what they were saying from a distance away. They hadn't been speaking in particularly low tones of voice, but it wasn't worth chancing it. They might need the element of surprise.

"Can you make it so he can't hear us?" April asked the girl.

"If you command it," the girl said levelly.

"I command you to make it so he cannot hear what we say."

The girl raised her hands above her head. Sand and dust from the surrounding ground that had only just settled after the houses had been moved now rose around them in a sphere, swirling and whirling. It was like being inside a reverse snow globe, except sand and rocks flew around them instead of fake snow.

"He can't hear us?" April asked. There was a low whirling sound, but it was low and gentle, like a fan running in a room.

"It's louder outside," The girl explained. "Loud enough to drown out our words. I made it so we can't hear it as much, but..."

She snapped her fingers, and the rest of her words were drowned out by the whirling sand. The sound was so loud that April and Dorian immediately covered their ears.

"Enough," April said, but her words didn't even make a dent through the noise. She waved her hand at the girl, who snapped her fingers again.

"Is it sufficient, Mistress?" she asked, her voice dripping with disdain.

Dorian leaned in to speak in April's ear. "I can see why the magician doesn't take her around with him," he said. He didn't bother to keep his voice low enough so that the girl couldn't hear him.

"Why should I not make his dominion over me all the harder?" The girl asked, her words venomous.

"How do we know that you'll cooperate with us if we agree to free you?" April asked. She crossed her arms. "How do we know that you won't try to make things difficult for us?"

The sarcastic look dropped from the girl's face. "I promise it, Mistress. Just free me from my bonds."

April considered the young girl. "The genie mentioned a binding verbal agreement," she said. "Do you know how to do that?"

The girl nodded earnestly. "We simply agree to our terms and then shake. A magically binding contract."

"Okay," April said, nodding. "We'll do that. But will you tell me your name first?"

The girl lowered her head. "I must tell you if you command me, but I would prefer not to. A djinni's name is a part of her power. We protect it fiercely."

She waited uncomfortably, tensely anticipating April's next move.

"I wouldn't want to force you to do anything you don't want," April said. "Why don't I call you Sapphire after your ring?"

The girl looked up, surprised. She didn't comment on April not forcing her to reveal her name, but there was something in her that relaxed, became less guarded. April hoped it was enough to build a little trust between them.

The girl nodded. "That would be fine."

It was a start. "You know the genie has been commanded to stop anyone who comes near that building by any means necessary. This includes killing them."

Sapphire's eyes flashed. "I am powerful. He cannot kill me."

April winced. In her experience, it was every djinni's M.O. to declare themselves the most powerful being in a room. She wasn't sure if each of them believed it, or if that was just their culture.

"You are obviously powerful," April said. It had been quite a show, surprising even the genie—but he'd also said that it wasn't enough to match him. She was inclined to believe this. She'd seen the genie do fantastical things, though never anything on the scale of rearranging a city block... but then again, he'd never had cause to.

April continued, "How many other genies have you ever fought in combat? Tell the truth—that's a command."

The girl looked down, her confidence faltering. "None," she said, but then she added quickly, "My friends and I used to play battle, before I was captured. I always won."

April couldn't help but smile. The girl was so inexperienced she didn't even realize *how* inexperienced she was. It was as endearing as it was foreboding.

Sapphire seemed eager to prove herself. "Don't worry, Mistress. I can easily kill the djinni of the red ring. You have nothing to fear."

April fought exasperation. "I don't want him to die, either."

Sapphire's eyes grew confused. "You don't?"

"No, I don't. I don't want anyone to die."

The girl bit her lip. "Killing him is the only way to ensure that he can't come back and throw more magic at us," she explained. "I really advise against keeping him alive."

"It's not negotiable," April said, her voice so hard that the girl looked away. *Damn it,* she cursed herself. She'd just used the power the ring gave her over the girl to her advantage. She couldn't let herself do that again. It was too icky.

She made her voice softer the next time she spoke. "Do you have any ideas of how to do that?"

The girl shook her head. Bless her, she had the heart of a warrior, but hadn't yet developed a mind for strategy.

"First thing," Dorian said. "That building he destroyed has a magical doorway in it. That's why Rottman forced him to destroy it—he doesn't want us to get through it."

Sapphire nodded. "I feel the power emanating from it. More than anything I've ever felt before." She looked at April earnestly. "It's connected to you, like a thread leads from it to wherever you stand."

April looked around herself as though she might see this thread. She always felt the gate when inside one of the books, but she didn't really get the sense of anything connecting her back to the portal.

"Do you think you can undo what he's done to the building?"

The girl's expression became grave as she shook her head. "Unfortunately not, Mistress," she said. "It would take a long time. As it is now, he will not let me anywhere near it. I hope you won't think less of my abilities."

She bowed her head silently.

"Of course not," April reassured her.

Dorian pursed his lips, deep in thought. "He might be expecting such a move, anyway. He'll assume you don't want to risk the girl's life."

"And he would be very correct in that assumption."

Dorian averted his eyes. "I would have suggested nothing else. I just want to make sure we're all the same page about what's about to happen here." He tilted his head towards the girl.

April took the hint. "Sapphire," she said. "I need you to promise me that you won't risk your life going up against the genie."

The girl's brow furrowed. "I must protest," she said. "I may need to do so in order to best him. He won't expect me to go after him directly. It gives me an advantage."

Her brow crinkled, and even though April knew that she'd never say so, she seemed to think it was an advantage she couldn't spare.

April shook her head. "It's not worth your life," she said.

Sapphire's expression grew angry. "I can decide if my freedom is worth my life or not."

April's brow furrowed, confused. "You get your freedom either way. Seems like a good reason to try to stay alive to me."

"You mean you'll grant me my freedom even if I fail?" Sapphire's eyes were narrowed, like someone who's just been offered a deal too good to be true by a sleazy car salesman.

"Here are my terms," April said, "One: Do your best to get us to the gate and keep the genie away from us long enough to see if we can get through the gate. Two: Do everything that I say, as long as it doesn't put you in danger. Three: If you even *think* that you might be in danger, you get out of there as fast as you can. He can teleport himself and others, so be aware of that."

Sapphire bit her lip. "He might be able to stop me from escaping," she admitted. Apparently her assurances had given the girl reason to trust her, because she was admitting a fault. "Some djinn can do that to each other sometimes if they time it right."

"He shouldn't do that," April said. "He doesn't *want* to hurt us—he's being forced to by Rottman's commands. He'll leave you alone as soon as you're not directly helping us."

Sapphire thought about this and nodded. "That makes sense." Her brow wrinkled. "Are you certain you want me to spare his life at all cost, even if his death meant we would achieve our goal?"

April nodded. "Yes, I'm sure. Do not harm him."

Dorian touched April's shoulder lightly. "Can I talk to you for a moment? In private?"

April nodded, and they stepped away. April noticed that they sphere of swirling dust widened to accommodate their move.

"I know you don't want to hurt him," Dorian said, his expression grave. "But I must urge you to consider the bigger picture. If we don't get back to the other side before the gate closes, we're all dead—including the genie and everyone else. It's your decision, but don't take it lightly."

Despite Dorian's sour mood the previous couple of hours, April knew he only said this because it was true. Still, she was silent for several moments before nodding. "But only if it's absolutely necessary," she said.

"Of course."

They stepped back over to Sapphire, who had a knowing look.

"You heard all that, didn't you?" April asked.

Sapphire nodded. "But you must command it."

This caused April to pause even longer. Then she nodded, a motion that was barely perceptible. "I give you permission to harm the genie. But only if you're absolutely positive that we'll get to the gate, and only if it's the only way." Not wanting to linger on these words lest she lose her nerve and take them back, she held out her hand. "Do we have a deal?" Her voice shook.

Without hesitating Sapphire reached out and took it. "I accept your terms," she said. "I will abide by your rules. Here are mine: once you are able to get to your gate—or when we know there is no chance of you getting there," she added hastily with an apologetic smile, "then my freedom will be automatically granted."

April started to pull her hand away, but then she held fast. She got the feeling that once the handshake was broken, the contract could not be amended. "And you're not allowed to use your powers to cause significant harm to others—unless it's in self-defense," she said. She hoped this wording would eliminate the risk of something similar to what had happened with the genie happening again.

Sapphire didn't blink at the additional rule, only nodded. "I accept." She pulled her hand away. A frisson of energy passed between them, sealing the deal. "What should I do, if you don't want me to attack him directly? It will be difficult to attack him if I want to minimize the risk of hurting him or take risk myself."

"Let's distract him," April said, and she laid out her plan.

Ten minutes later the cyclone of sand moved behind them, spreading out into a wall that curved around all sides of the buildings ringing them, and the world seemed suddenly quiet without its constant droning hum so close. April's ears rang as she looked around for the genie. He stood in the same place he'd been in when Sapphire had called the cyclone forth, as though he hadn't moved at all.

His already-tense jaw hardened even more. "Make it good," he said.

April nodded to the forms standing beside her. Sapphire looked like herself, but the form of Dorian was dark and murky—a decoy. The real Dorian was running behind the wall of sand, out of the genie's line of sight. The fake Dorian stood behind them near the wall. Hopefully the swirling sand would distort him so that the genie wouldn't notice that he was only a shadow of the real Dorian.

April sent out a silent thought of support to the real Dorian. She'd wanted to be the one to make the journey towards the gate, but Dorian had protested, of course. He'd said that the genie would pay more attention to her. April had to admit he was right—the genie would notice right away if they tried to make a decoy of herself.

So she'd sent Dorian into the danger zone, like a general deploying soldiers from the safety of a distant hilltop. That's how Randall would see it, anyway. Pain developed in her chest as she thought of Randall. She wished that he were here.

They stood for thirty seconds, stalling. She hoped the genie would think that she was having doubts.

He opened his mouth. "You must attack, Sorceress," he said. "I cannot let you stay there forever. It's best if you make the first move."

He gritted his teeth with the effort of stopping himself from doing something. The space between the wall of dust and the buildings curved around them was mounded with sand and dirt; it would take Dorian some time to get over them.... But they'd stalled as long as they could. April nodded to Sapphire. "As we discussed."

Sapphire nodded back, then turned her attention on the genie. She raised her hand, the gesture grandiose, and another cyclone of earth lifted from the earth a dozen feet in front of him. His eyes widened as it barreled towards him, and at the last moment it lifted him into the air. He spiraled around the vortex for a few seconds before being thrown away from it—he was now further from the fallen building, which was good. The spiral changed trajectory, now targeting his new location. He rose to his feet. He waved his hand and it dissipated before it got to him.

April checked Sapphire's expression. She looked worried. From their talks earlier, she'd said that the genie would be able to dispel this attack, but from her expression it seemed that she hadn't expected him to do it so quickly.

She pursed her lips and made the same sweeping gestures with each of her hands, and two more cyclones picked up. They barreled towards the genie, but he waved his hands and first one and then the other fell away.

"Do better," he yelled through gritted teeth.

Over his shoulder, Dorian appeared from behind the curtain of swirling sand. The effect had only reached so closely to the building; Sapphire had explained that the genie had placed the djinn version of a ward over it. Dorian had made it there, but he'd need to check the gate out in the open.

She needed to distract the genie. He'd already started to turn slightly back towards the building. If he saw Dorian...

She stepped towards the edge of the alley. In her mind's eye she pictured a line extending out from the edge of the last building. If she crossed it, the genie would attack her.

Her ploy worked. Even though she hadn't yet crossed the line, he turned towards her, his back now to Dorian.

"Don't," the genie said.

Dorian fumbled with something, struggling to lift a large piece of rubble that had once been a wall. He needed more time.

April took another step forward. The toe of her right foot was even with the imaginary line, millimeters from exiting the no fire zone.

"Mistress, don't," Sapphire said.

April ignored the plea. "Whatever happens, help Dorian," she said, unsure if Sapphire would still help them if she was dead. April thought she might. She lifted her left foot and stepped over the line, then the right foot. She kept walking. Her eyes moving between Dorian and the genie. Dorian was framed so perfectly above the genie's broad shoulders that the genie would assume she was looking at him...

Nothing happened right away. April wondered if the man who'd told them where the safety line was had been had been off by a few feet. Or maybe the genie's power needed to charge, or maybe he was fighting it.

Whatever it was, after she took three steps, she instinctively felt the blast coming for her. She turned at the last possible moment so that the strike hit her from behind, mostly on her right side.

She cried out as heat erupted against the right side of her back, her shoulder taking the brunt of the force.

"Mistress!" Sapphire called, and moments later April stood back on the safe side of the line. Sapphire must have teleported her there.

This thought was quickly overshadowed by the searing pain. It felt so hot, like a thousand fire ants were swarming her right shoulder, each biting down with acid-coated pincers.

She glanced down at the screaming limb and saw that her t-shirt was singed, and had even burned away in spots so that she could see her reddened skin. It blistered before her eyes.

She hissed as the crawling, burning pain started. Nausea roiled in her gut, but she ignored it. Her stomach was empty, anyway. What was it that Gram always said to do with a burn? Put ice on it before it blisters. It was too late for that, even if there was ice in this desert.

"Mistress," Sapphire said. Without asking permission she stepped over to her and placed her hand on the burn.

"Ahh!" The searing pain intensified beneath her palm, but in a few moments it cooled and faded. Sapphire pulled her hand away. The flesh was puckered and scarred, but the wound no longer looked raw; it had scabbed over. The girl had somehow quickened the healing process.

"That's as much as I can do," she said. "I've never been much of a healer."

"It's perfect," April said. She brushed her fingers over her shoulder experimentally. Tendrils of pain shivered across the damaged flesh. It felt like a massage compared to what it had been before. She could live with this—and more importantly, she could fight like this.

She turned back towards the genie. His eyes smoldered as she watched him. She could still see Dorian behind him—he'd stopped trying to lift the giant slab of wall; it must have been too heavy. He picked up smaller rocks that must have covered a different section of the gate.

Then she felt it—a tiny bit of the gate breaking free. A pressure she hadn't realized had been weighing on her spine lifted slightly. It decreased, she imagined, with every rock that Dorian was managing to pull away from the gate's face.

"He's done it," she said. "He's uncovered the gate." She could sense via her connection with the gate that the opening was not yet large enough for any of them to slip through, but it was widening quickly.

She wasn't the only one who felt the change. Maybe the genie also could feel what was going on with the gate behind him, or maybe he'd heard her words. Either way, he furrowed his brow, suddenly suspicious, and turned. His back was turned to April when he saw Dorian, but she saw the heat-wave magic coming off of his body increase.

He lifted his hand. April opened her mouth to call for him to stop. It wouldn't do any good, but the reaction was so visceral that she couldn't stop it. It never left her mouth.

Dorian was pulled backwards through the air, out away from the ruined building. As he was pulled, his left heel collided with the edge of the fallen wall he'd been trying to move earlier. April was too far away to hear the crunch of bone—it would have been drowned out by the wall of dust behind them, anyway—but she saw the strange, painful angle his foot suddenly pointed in.

He landed on the ground halfway between her and the genie, his foot still twisted out at that impossible direction, his soft leather boot turned awkwardly so he'd almost be able to see its bottom.

"Dorian!" she screamed. Without thinking, she ran forward towards him, kneeling down on the ground.

"Are you okay?" she said. It had only been a few seconds, but the leather of his boot had grown taught as the flesh inside it swelled. *We need to cut the boot off,* she thought, her mind grasping at the first aid class she'd taken in high school, *before his circulation gets cut off...*

That was the least of their worries. She felt a wave of heat building towards them. She'd seen what it had done to those other men. They'd lived because they'd been able to run away before the blast happened. Dorian couldn't run.

"Go," Dorian croaked, his face twisted in pain. "Whatever happens, you'll need to take me back to my study."

He said the word *me,* but what he really meant was his body, because if she left him there, the genie would kill him. He smiled apologetically.

"I can't leave you," she said.

"You must," he croaked. The air around them was hot. It had been hot before, almost unbearably so, but now it was the temperature of an oven.

"But then you'll be dead," she said. "And you're a main character. Won't that break your world?" she asked, desperate for a reason to save him, feeling the hopelessness of not being able to either way.

"My world was broken long ago," he said. "Go."

"He's right," the genie said. When she looked up he stood behind them, close enough that she could reach out and touch the edge of his silk pants. "The only reason you're still alive is that I'm controlling it, and you're not currently trying to get to the gate. But I can only keep it up for so long." His face was twisted in that pained look of control. He was fighting a losing battle.

April stood. She couldn't leave Dorian.

"The only reason you're able to control it so much is because I'm standing here," she said, repeating the genie's own words back to him. It was painful to speak, and her eyes itched as the oven-like air robbed them of their moisture. "If I leave now, Dorian would die. You don't care about him like you care about me."

The genie didn't accept her words. He didn't have to. "He'll die either way," he said. "If you stay here, he will only die a slower, more agonizing death—as you will. The quickness of fire is a kindness compared to dehydration."

"I can't just leave him."

"Then you will perish," the djinni said. "If I were a stronger man, I would incinerate you and be done with it. I'm sorry."

The heat pushed in on all sides. Even if she ran now, she wasn't sure she'd make it. She knelt next to Dorian. Every breath she took felt like fire.

"This is a foolish thing you've done," Dorian chided her. His skin was stretched over his cheeks, making him look like a sick old man. Was this what his portrait looked like?

"Do you really want the last thing you say to me to be an admonishment?" she asked. "I suppose it's fitting."

He smiled, and as he did so his lips cracked. The blood that welled out dried to a rust-colored powder almost as soon as it hit the air. "I already said everything I wanted to say to you the last time we were about to die."

April knew exactly what he was talking about. He'd told her how he felt about her. Of course, he'd immediately shut down any chance she'd had to say how *she* felt. Even as she was about to die, even though she wasn't sure how she felt, this irked her. Why did he get to dictate how their relationship went? Didn't she get a say in the matter?

Her own lips cracked, and she licked at the sharp flesh, her tongue hungry for any bit of moisture it could get, even if it had to cannibalize her own blood to get it.

"But you never... let me.... Say... how I..." she said, the last words escaping from her mouth in a puff. Even her throat was cracking as she spoke. She didn't think she could say more.

Dorian looked confused, then his eyes widened. If he wanted to hear more than that, he wasn't going to. Her voice had dried out. The skin of his face had begun to pull away from his eyes at the corners. He now looked less like an old man and more like a corpse.

She reached out and took his hand, grasping it, hating how brittle it felt. She closed her eyes and prepared to die. She hoped that whatever the afterlife looked like, it would be cold there. And with lots of water, and ice, and diet soda...

She felt herself being swirled up; Dorian's hand pulled out of her grasp. She felt disgruntled at the fact that they couldn't go together. Did she have to go through the dying process alone? Would they even go to the same heaven? How did the whole interdimensional death thing work, anyway?

It was definitely cooler, but not by much. Still, she wouldn't complain. What she hadn't expected was the spinning—and the stinging on her face, and anywhere on her body that she had skin exposed. And why did she still feel so thirsty? It felt unfair that one had to be thirsty in heaven.

She opened her eyes, then immediately closed them after they were bombarded by whipping sand. She blinked, but her body was so dehydrated that there weren't any tears to dislodge the particles. She was inside the cyclone, she realized.

Sapphire? Had the djinn girl gotten them out somehow?

As soon as the thought entered her head, she felt herself being pulled out of the whirlwind and back into the heat—though it was not as hot as it had been before. Now it was just highly uncomfortable, especially as dehydrated as she was.

She opened her burning eyes to tiny slits. Dorian was sprawled next to her, wincing as his broken ankle landed in an unfortunate position.

"Are you okay?" she asked. Her voice had returned slightly, but she sounded like she had one hell of a cold. She wondered if Sapphire had healed them a little while they were in the whirlwind.

"I'm definitely not okay," Dorian said. If Sapphire had healed them, she definitely hadn't done anything to Dorian's broken ankle. "But alive."

There was a pop in the empty space to her right, and the air momentarily picked up. The breeze might have felt nice, if it hadn't been accompanied by a face full of sand, and if April's skin wasn't so raw and uncomfortable.

Sapphire tumbled out of the air as the whirlwind retaliated. She landed on her backside, looking confused. The girl's eyes widened as the genie stepped closer to them.

"Stupid girl," he growled. It took April a second to realize he wasn't talking to her, he was talking to Sapphire.

Concerned for the girl's safety, April said, "Sapphire, get out of here. You've done your job. Your freedom is yours."

Sapphire moved her hands through the air shakily. The motions lacked the grace and confidence they'd possessed earlier. She looked even more frightened. "I can't."

"She tried to transport you next to the gate," the genie explained. His face was stone-hard, as though trying to separate himself from what he was about to do.

"I told you to get out of here if things looked bad," April said.

"You are a good woman, Mistress," Sapphire said, looking down, "unlike most of the humans I have met. I could not let you die in such a brutal way."

"May we learn never to get attached to humans," The genie shook his head. "Your plan might have worked, if you had taken them *away* from the gate rather than trying to get them closer to it. That is a lesson a more experienced djinni would have known. I can't let you go, now. The trick bought you a few minutes, but nothing more."

The air began to get hot again. April felt panic rise in her chest, having just escaped this situation only to be brought right back into it. She wondered why the genie didn't just take his own advice and incinerate them. He was a coward for making them suffer.

April fought the panic. At least Dorian was here. She regretted that the others weren't here. Randall, Thaddeus, and Gram...

She blinked. Gram? For a moment she swore that she'd seen Gram's familiar silver perm floating beyond the genie's dome of heat magic. A hallucination, no doubt. Funny—she would have expected Gram to be smiling and welcoming her with open arms, or at least standing up. Definitely not unconscious, slung over a donkey.

The donkey was one step to far. April sat up. It was one of the hardest, most painful things she'd ever done. "Gram?" she asked, and she felt not only her lips split, but also the apples of her cheeks and the place where her nostrils met her upper lip.

It *was* Gram, and she was slung over a donkey. She looked to her left—Dorian looked unconscious, or maybe dead. To her right, Sapphire's face was twisted in pain. She looked better than Dorian (and herself, she supposed). She hadn't suffered through the first spell of heat, after all. The girl was closest to Gram.

"Sapphire," April said, her vocal cords feeling like they, too, were splitting open.

The girl looked over at her, frightened.

Not wanting to waste the little moisture left in her throat, April pointed to Gram.

Sapphire followed the line of her finger, then looked back to April, confusion mixing with the pained expression on her face.

"Ring," April tried to say, but nothing came out. She formed her thumb and index finger into a loop, then brought it down over the middle finger of her opposite hand. The webbing between her fingers split. The impromptu sign language must have been enough, because looked to Gram's hand, where the genie's red ring was.

Her heat-stroked brain struggled to piece together what had happened. Gram and Thaddeus must have overpowered Rottman somehow, then they'd managed to come through on a different page. The magic touch the genie had placed on Gram to temporarily relieve her symptoms must have worn of...

But where was Thaddeus? Why would he send Gram through on her own? It didn't make sense. It seemed like the most obvious answer was that Gram was a strange hallucination.

April lay her head back on the dirt. She tried to close her eyes, but they were too dehydrated; her upper eyelids didn't meet the lower ones. She watched through the slivered gaps between them as Sapphire crawled over to Gram. Maybe Gram was real, after all... not that it mattered, now. There was no way Sapphire could get past the genie's hold... she struggled even to move the tiniest bit. She'd never get the ring.

The donkey continued to walk towards them, until Gram's hand pierced through the edge of the heat magic. Sapphire reached out towards it...

April rooted for the girl, even though it was too late to do anything. *Go, go, go...*

Sapphire's fingers brushed Grams for only a moment. As expected, nothing happened for several moments... but then Gram stirred. Sapphire had head Gram.

April felt outside of herself as she watched Gram sit up. She didn't look as spry as when the genie had healed her, but she was awake. She glanced over at Sapphire, her eyes widening. Then her eyes fell on April, then Dorian.

She turned toward the genie and spoke. April couldn't hear the words, maybe because she was no longer in her body. Gram lifted the ring, brandishing it.

The heat dissipated, and April was suddenly in her body again. She immediately wished she wasn't. Everything hurt, and she craved nothing more than to fall into a glacial spring and drink until her body burst.

She felt hot, burning hands on her. She flinched away from them, but then she heard the genie's voice. "I'm going to help you."

She still recoiled from his touch, but was too weak to fight him off. The heat of his magic burned through her, but this time it restored rather than destroyed.

When she felt well enough that she wasn't in danger of immediate death, she pushed him away. "Help Dorian," she said. She glanced over at Sapphire. She must have healed herself, because she was already standing. She looked miserable, but not in immediate peril.

Dorian, however, still lay on the ground. He hadn't moved even after the genie's magic was gone.

"Is he..." she trailed off, unable to finish the sentence.

The genie didn't respond. He knelt down by Dorian's form, his brow furrowed and his lips tight. This, more than anything else, assured her of Dorian's death. If he'd even been breathing, the genie would have made some disparaging remark about him.

He placed his hands on Dorian's chest. For nearly a minute, nothing happened. April watched, her heart sinking further and further into despair. He couldn't be dead. All the universes of the gate could not stretch to accommodate such a thing.

"April," Gram wheezed, "Come here..."

April went and stood by Gram, who was using the donkey as a crutch to lean on. In her other hand she clutched a long stick, using it to balance herself. April wrapped her arms around her, ignoring the pain on her arms as they pressed into Gram. She must have second-degree burns there.

"I'm so sorry, hon," Gram said, wheezing between each word.

April's eyes felt like they were going to cry, but there was no moisture to produce tears. If Gram was saying she was sorry, it really meant that he was gone.

She saw the black splotches of ink rot covering Gram's hand and the genie's ring. Numbly, she reached out and ran her fingers over it. The rot immediately turned to dust. A breeze billowed by, carrying the dust with it. April watched it blow away until it became indistinguishable from the smoke billowing around them from the remains of the fire. As long as she watched it, she wouldn't have to think about Dorian...

Behind them came a moan, not deep enough to belong to the genie.

"He's alive," the genie said. He sounded relieved. He pulled his hands away. "I healed him enough to stabilize him," he said. "But I would imagine he doesn't want to be fully healed by me."

Dorian groaned again. "You're damn right about that," he said, "But if someone could help me up... my ankle is still broken." His voice croaked, but he sounded better than could be expected for someone who had been practically dead only moments before.

April hurried to help him up. The genie tried to help as well, but Dorian swatted his hand away. Normally this would have annoyed her, but now she only cared that Dorian was alive. When he stood upright, she was able to get a good look at his face. His usually perfect skin was chapped and sunburned. A blood vessel had burst in one of his eyes, tinging the white a splotchy, pinkish red.

Unable to quell her immediate reaction, April gasped.

"You don't look so good yourself," he said wryly. No one laughed at the joke.

Gram held out the long stick. "Here... use this."

Dorian propped the stick under his arm gratefully.

"I'll get some water," Sapphire said, and she walked towards a nearby well and started pulling on the rope that was tied to the end.

April glanced around her. She felt like the battle was over, but it wasn't, was it?

She looked at Gram. "Where's Thaddeus? What happened with Rottman?"

Gram's face darkened. "Thaddeus is... with him. We couldn't leave him... alone."

"Thaddeus needs us," April said. She turned towards the fallen house. "We should get back to him."

Gram nodded. "I came in through a different page, but he said he'd flip the page back to this one as soon as I was through."

Sapphire came back carrying a clay pot of water and handed it to April.

She held it out to Dorian, but he shook his head. "You first."

She didn't need to be told twice. She lifted the pot to her mouth. The water tasted like dirt, metallic and grainy, and she could see sediment in the bottom of the vessel. It was still the best water she'd ever had. She finished half of it before handing it off to Dorian.

He held it out to Gram, but she shook her head, and wheezed, "If you don't drink... right now, I'll break your... other leg..."

Dorian waved his hand to silence her. "Fine, as long as you keep quiet. You need to save your strength." He drained the pot. When he finished he frowned into its depths as though it had something offensive written on the bottom. "Unfortunately, the gate has been pretty well covered. I'd say that's at least ten feet of rubble. I could only uncover the very edge of the door, and not enough that any of us could squeeze through."

"I can fix that," the genie said. "Stand back."

He swept his arms wide, and the remainder of the house lifted up, rearranging itself into piles. He waved his arm again, and bits of rubble and wood pulled up, coming together until they formed a doorway. Behind it shimmered the library.

Rottman sat in a chair, Thaddeus sat across from him. He looked as though he'd just seen a ghost. Rottman smiled at Thaddeus. There was something different about his face; something that hadn't been there the last time she'd seen him. She was too far away to make out exactly what was happening, though, especially through the shimmering barrier of the veil.

Gram sighed with relief. "Thank God he's all right."

Despite Gram's sentiment, April wasn't sure that that was the case. Thaddeus looked terrified, and there was something else bothering her. It took her a moment to put her finger on what it was, but then she finally realized: it was fear. Not hers, not Thaddeus', but the gate's. The gate was frightened.

"I have to help them," April said. She walked to the veil.

"Them?" Gram said behind her, confused, but April didn't take the time to respond.

She passed through the veil, and Thaddeus looked over at her, surprised. Had he not noticed that the world on the other side had righted itself? Time did move faster on the book side of the veil; maybe it had all happened in the blink of an eye.

"April?" he said. His eyes widened. "Are you all right?"

She nodded. She must look pretty bad, and she felt like she'd spent hours out in the sun without sunscreen. But she was alive, and that seemed pretty all right to her.

"How's everything here?" She asked, looking at Rottman. Thaddeus must have him magically bound, because he wasn't moving away from the chair. His wrists and feet were pressed together as though bound by invisible handcuffs. Despite this, his posture was relaxed.

Now that she was closer, Thaddeus looked even more terrified. Perspiration glistened from his forehead, and his face looked white. The muscles stuck out in his cheeks and neck. He gripped the wand in his right hand, his knuckles white.

She'd seen him in a similar state before—when he was out of his mind after consuming the gate's threshold, and whenever he'd had an episodic break from reality thereafter. He looked more lucid, though; not like he was watching a film on a screen that no one else could see.

"We need to kill it," he said without further explanation. He held his hand out towards her.

It? She hesitated. Wouldn't it be better to question Rottman before destroying him? First they needed to figure out what he'd been planning. He'd gone through a lot of trouble and April couldn't see what he was getting out of it.

But the longer they kept him around, the more likely it was that he was going to escape. April was surprised that Thaddeus was able to keep concentration enough to keep him bound in his frightened state as it was. And he would know that there was no way they'd keep him alive—what incentive did he have to answer their questions truthfully, anyway?

More than that, April felt repulsed by the thing smiling at her from the chair across the table, it's glistening oil-slick skin almost reflecting her face back at her. She felt the gate's panic, like the frantic flutter of a bird's wings as it sits on your shoulder. The gate wanted him destroyed, but it also seemed to know that such a thing was impossible. Sure, she and Thaddeus could make the hateful creature in front of them disappear with a touch, but he'd rebuild himself elsewhere in the collection.

She nodded, then took Thaddeus' hand. Dorian stepped through the gate, with the genie close behind him. Gram must have taken a little longer due to her slow walk-speed.

With the others watching and Thaddeus holding her left hand, she reached out and touched Rottman. He never stopped smiling, even as he dried out and flaked away.

The genie waved away the particles as they dispersed. "Good riddance."

"He'll be back." Thaddeus' voice was soft, dangerous.

"What do you mean?" Dorian asked, leaning on his crutch.

Thaddeus looked up at them. "We did the same thing to him before. He's going to come back again."

"He's right," April said, thinking of the smile on his face as she touched him. It wasn't the expression of a man who was about to die. He'd expected this, had *wanted* it, even. But why?

"Did he say anything to you?" April asked Thaddeus. She wished they'd been able to question him, though she was still sure that he wouldn't have answered any of their questions truthfully.

"Not much," Thaddeus said. "But... he changed."

April nodded. "Yeah. He was a lot bigger and dumber the last time we ran into him."

Thaddeus shook his head. "No. I mean, yes, he was, but that's not what I'm talking about. *He changed in front of me.* At first it was just little flashes. His skin would look like human skin, but it was so quick that I thought I was seeing things. But then he *really* changed. He turned into you, and Randall, and me. I looked the most realistic. I think that's because he's spent the most time with me."

"He can shapeshift?" Dorian asked. "Are you sure?"

"You're telling me he can change his face?" Gram asked. She'd stepped in after the genie just in time to see Rottman disperse.

Thaddeus nodded gravely.

"That can't be possible," Dorian said.

"Why not?" April asked. "We know he's changed from a giant monster into a believably human shape. Who's to say he isn't refining that ability?"

She thought of what that meant. He could look like anyone. What if he decided to come after them again? They'd never see it coming.

"I think it will take him time to reform himself," Thaddeus said. "That's something that's going for us, at least."

April bit her lip. "Why did he do all this?" she asked. The question had been bothering her ever since Rottman confronted them at the gate. "What did he want?"

"Whatever it was, he failed," Dorian said.

Thaddeus shook his head. "I don't think so." He paused. "I think being here made him stronger. Gave him more information. He gets something from our world that he doesn't get from the books."

April closed her eyes. She didn't want to deal with any of this right now. She'd almost died. Going home and resting seemed reasonable.

"Why don't we talk about it tomorrow?" she said, and suddenly swayed. Both Dorian and the genie reached for her, but she grabbed the nearest table to steady herself.

As everyone nodded in agreement, they heard footsteps echoing up the staircase. April heard the jingle of Rex's collar before she turned around.

Randall stood in the doorway. His eyes were wide as he took in all of them. "No one texted me, so I figured you were all still here," he said. His face narrowed in concern when he took in first April's appearance and then Dorian's. "What the hell happened? You look like you've been through the fires of hell—literally. And is your foot broken?" his eyes shifted to the genie. "And what are you doing here?"

April sighed. Her hopes for a quick exit home were diminishing. "Do you guys mind explaining things to him?" She asked. "And maybe you can look at Dorian's ankle." Randall knew basic first aid from his time in the army. If the fracture was simple enough, he might even be able to set it... if not, April didn't know how they were going to fit in a trip to the hospital in the next couple of hours before the gate closed and Dorian needed to be safely in his study. Dorian had refused to let either Sapphire or the genie heal his ankle.

They all nodded. April was about to turn towards the genie, but Gram seemed to have similar ideas. She held up the ring. "What am I supposed to do with this?"

"I don't know," April said, too tired to make any more delegations. "You're the master of the ring. What do you want to do? If we keep the ring on this side, we have to send something of equal importance over there."

She bit her lip. She didn't even know if they had any items that were as powerful as a djinni ring. The closest thing was probably the wand—and they certainly weren't leaving that over there.

Gram thought for a moment. "I guess I grant you your freedom," she said, and the tattoo bands on his wrists faded.

"Thank you," he said, inspecting the newly unmarked skin. "I'm in your debt."

"Don't mention it." She held the ring out to the genie, but April swiped it before he was able to get to it.

"Bad things happened the last time we left this in your possession," she said.

The genie crossed his arms. "If you hadn't noticed, your grandmother didn't place the same restrictions on me as you did. There's no chance for me to mess it up."

Gram looked worried. Her eyes darted to April. "Did I do it wrong?" she said.

April shook her head. "The restriction didn't work out the first time," she said. She turned to the genie. "And I think you're all show with your death-to-man talk." She'd seen how much hurting those men had bothered him.

The genie raised an eyebrow but didn't respond.

"Oh! That reminds me. You're supposed to go set the genie of the cobalt ring free. We sort of promised him that when he let us go get Sapphire's ring."

She didn't mention that she'd also promised to make it a condition of the genie's freedom. He didn't need to know that.

The genie's eyes flashed momentarily, but then he nodded. "If you wish it, Sorceress. I owe you, after all."

A round face peered through the gate inquisitively.

"Sapphire," April said, and she stepped through to talk with the girl. The genie followed.

"Mistress," Sapphire addressed her. She bowed her head.

"None of that mistress crap." April shook her head. "My name's April. Would have told you sooner, if we hadn't been fighting for our lives." She paused, growing serious. "You saved us back there, even though you didn't have to. Thank you."

"It was nothing." Sapphire looked at the ground shyly. She looked more like a schoolgirl now, if you ignored the fire that occasionally flared up in her eyes. April imagined her walking down the hallways of a school and smiled. She would run the place.

But school—at least a modern one—wasn't in the cards for Sapphire. What would become of her?

"I thought you'd be long gone by now," April said. "Did our contract not work?"

"It worked," Sapphire said. She lifted her wrists to show that the tattoo-like bands were gone. "I just don't really have anywhere else to be."

"I thought you had a family?"

Sapphire nodded. "I do, but I don't know where to find them. I was dormant in my ring when the magician brought me to this city. I will need a place to stay while I search for them."

"That reminds me." April pulled the tiny ring from her pinkie and held it out to Sapphire.

After a moment's hesitation, Sapphire took it. "Thank you."

April glanced at the genie. "Why don't you stay with the genie? He owes you, anyway."

The genie looked startled by the proposition, but then nodded. "Asima could use some help. I'm sure she'd be happy to have you on."

April nodded. "Perfect." She met the genie's eyes. She needed privacy for what she was about to say to him. "Sapphire, do you mind if the genie and I talk alone?"

"Of course, mist—April," Sapphire corrected herself. "Do you think I might walk through your door and see what's on the other side?"

April nodded. "There's nothing interesting over there, though," she said, but then thought maybe that wasn't the case. The library must seem as fantastic to Sapphire as the genie's city did to April.

Sapphire stepped eagerly through the gate. April heard the others' greetings and words of welcome distorted through the veil.

The genie looked down at her, wincing like a puppy about to be hit. "What do you want to talk about?"

She breathed out. "I want you to know I don't blame you for what happened. Rottman would have found a way to get to us no matter what. You just happened to be the path that he chose. I'm sorry that he took advantage of you. I know how much you hate being under someone else's control." She paused. "I also wanted to thank you."

He inclined his head. "For?"

"For doing your best to fight his orders. If you hadn't, we'd be dead. And for always being there for me. My life's been crazy since I first stepped through the gate. You were something that I could hold onto." She stopped talking, and silence filled the air.

The genie picked up on the fact that she hadn't quite finished what she was going to say. "But?" His eyes were sad.

"But I can't see you anymore. What you did was manipulative, and it put all of us in danger, including yourself."

He breathed out. "You're right."

"I am?"

"Everything you said is correct. What you didn't say is that you are also bad for me. I made a terrible, foolish, embarrassing mistake in trying to lure you back to my side."

She nodded. "That's very mature of you."

He smirked. "I'm older than the sands, and you talk to me about maturity." His expression grew serious. He reached down and picked up a handful of pebbles from the ground. He pressed them between his palms. Heat and smoke escaped from the edges. When he was finished, he held out his hand so she could see what was there. The tiny pebbles now resembled embers. They shimmered and dimmed in vermillion red, orange, and black.

He tipped them into her hand. She expected them to burn, but they were only warm.

"For your grandmother," he said. "Each one will have the same effect as my touch did today," he explained. "All she has to do is eat one. It is impressive that she made it across the city today. A woman with that much heart deserves some reprieve."

"I can't take these back with me. It will upset the balance."

"It's fine, as long as you give me a similarly significant item in return, right?"

She nodded. What could she give him? She had an idea. It was perfect, but it made her tear up. "I think I have just the thing."

"What?"

"You'll see." April nodded to the stones. "Thank you," She shouldn't accept presents from the genie, but they would really help Gram.

He inclined his head slightly. "I only wish that I could do more." He paused. "May we share one last kiss?"

"That's not appropriate," April said, aware that the others—including Gram—could still see them through the gate. "But how about a hug?"

He looked disappointed, but nodded. It felt strange to put her arms around his neck. Her vision blurred. She knew this was for the best, but she was still tearing up. The genie, despite his flaws, meant a lot to her.

Before she could move away, he whispered in his ear, "My name is..." and told her his name. It was a nice name, though she felt no power in it. Still, it was at that moment that the tears actually slipped out of her eyes. She nodded, and pulled away.

The genie saw the moisture on her cheeks before she could turn away. He reached out and erased each tear with the pad of his thumb. "Don't cry," he said. "It's for the best."

"You're *happy* that I'm crying, aren't you?" she said, trying to smile.

"No." he said, but his smile widened.

"Liar."

"I suppose it assures me that you care," he admitted.

She nodded, and then, because she needed a way to break the tension, she said, "My name's April. Since you told me yours."

"I already knew that, Sorceress."

She shrugged. "Just making sure."

They stood awkwardly for a few more seconds before she turned towards the gate, making a small half-wave with one hand. "Well, bye."

"Not so fast. What's your trade for the stones?" His voice was impatient, curious.

She smiled. "I'll go get it."

She stepped back through, then turned to Sapphire. "He's waiting for you."

Sapphire nodded. She bit her lip before throwing her arms around April's neck. "Thank you, mis—I mean, *April.*"

The hug lasted a fraction of a second, then with a small wave to the others she disappeared through the portal. April watched her leave. At least she'd gotten one djinni to call her by name.

She walked towards the table where *One Thousand and One Nights* lay open. She gently pulled the leaf of pages containing the story of Aladdin and the lamp free from the binding, careful to keep the current page open.

Once it pulled free, the gate hissed in protest, confused because more than one page was open at a time. April reached down and flipped the book shut. The gate quieted.

April walked back to the gate. The genie waited just on the other side. If he recognized the significance of the pages in her hands, he didn't show it. Her eyes must have been red, because his forehead knit with worry when his eyes met hers.

"There's no need for sorrow, Sorceress. I'll be here if you need me."

She smiled. "No, you won't."

Before she could change her mind, she thrust the pages through into his hands. He took them, confused. His eyes widened with realization when the gate began to hiss and close.

She pulled her hands back through the veil, holding his gaze until it closed. There was time for him to throw the pages back through, but he didn't. He only nodded once.

After nearly twenty seconds, the gate closed completely, and she faced a solid wall. She wiped her eyes before turning back to the others.

"You okay, hon?" Gram asked, breathing shallowly between each word, but it was better than it had been. Of course Gram would notice her tears, despite the genie's attempt to wipe them away.

April nodded, trying to smile. "I'll be fine, Gram." she turned to Randall, Thaddeus, and Dorian. Dorian sat with his leg propped up on two chairs, his swollen ankle elevated by a stack of books. The first aid kit lay open on the table between them, single serving packets of ibuprofen and packs of gauze littering the table.

"Janet's going to start wondering what's happened to all the first aid supplies," April joked, and the other's laughed, happy for the break in tension. The only one who didn't was Dorian, who watched her with concern.

"The fracture looks clean, which is good," Randall explained. "I made a makeshift splint with rulers from the supply cabinet, then wrapped it."

"It hurt like the Dickens," Dorian said, finally breaking eye contact. He looked pale despite his heat-burned skin.

Randall clapped him on the shoulder and Dorian winced. April could relate. Almost every part of her body hurt.

"We have to keep an eye on it," Randall said. "If it doesn't show signs of healing, or looks like it might set crooked, we need to take him to the hospital."

"Here," Thaddeus said, handing each of them a cup of water. April drank hers gratefully. She wished she'd made the genie heal her and Dorian fully before sending him off. But that felt too much like using him, and anyway Dorian would never accept help from the genie.

Speaking of the genie's healing powers... "Here, Gram," she said, and held out her palm.

Gram looked confused but allowed April to pour the shimmering stones into her hand. "What are these?" She was able to get the words out without gasping for breath, but coughed a little after.

"A gift from the genie," April said after the coughs subsided. "They'll help you, just like his touch did. It's temporary, of course, but nice to have around."

"It was the best feeling in the world to feel healthy again." Gram stared down at the stones, worrying one with her fingers. She was silent for so long that April thought she'd been hypnotized by them. She was about to ask if she was okay when Gram lifted her hand over the nearest wastepaper basket, releasing the stones in a steady stream.

"What are you doing? Those could help you!"

"It was the best feeling in the world," Gram said, her voice a little stronger, "But it was fake. I felt the disease lingering below the surface. And coming down from that was hard. Anyway, that man used the same magic to hurt you."

"He didn't have a choice, Gram."

"I know, and I feel sorry for him. I even forgive him. But I don't want any part of the magic that almost took you away from me." She placed her hand gently on April's cheek. Then her expression hardened. "And I don't want to hear another word about it."

She started to cough again, the fit spurred on by the intensity of her words.

April glanced at the others. None of them looked at Gram head-on. No one wanted to upset her more than she already was.

"Is it always life or death around here?" Gram asked.

"Sometimes. Though this is about as life or death as it comes." She paused. "We can talk about all that tomorrow. I think for now we should get home."

It wasn't difficult to convince everyone it was time to head home for the night. Out in the parking lot, she made sure to get Gram settled in the car before exclaiming, "Darn, I left my phone in my office. Do you mind if I run up and grab it?"

Gram waved her off. "I might be asleep by the time you get back down here," she said, her eyes fighting to stay open. "You go on, now."

"We'll wait with her until you get back," Thaddeus said, and his eyes skimmed the edge of the parking lot. April didn't have to ask who he was looking for. Silvis and The Collectors were still out there, biding their time. But that was a problem for another night.

"Thanks," April said, and a lump formed in her throat, suddenly aware of just how good it was to have Randall and Thaddeus around. "For everything. If it weren't for you guys…"

She wrapped them in a hug, one arm around each of their necks. Randall patted her back, but Thaddeus stiffened, clearing his throat.

"Right," she said, pulling away. "I'll just be a minute."

April took the stairs two at a time. She grabbed her cell phone off her desk where she'd purposefully left it, then stepped over to the wastepaper basket where Gram had tossed the genie's magic stones.

Carefully, she picked each and every one out of the garbage. Luckily the garbage had been changed shortly before the library closed, so there wasn't anything else in there. She counted as she picked them up—seven in total.

"April?"

She looked up to see Dorian. He leaned unsteadily against the table, keeping the weight off of his ankle. She opened her palm so he could see the stones. "I'm collecting these," she said, then checked the can to make sure she hadn't missed any.

"Did Gram change her mind?"

"Of course not," April said. "But these could come in handy later," she said. What if Rottman came back? And they might offer Gram some relief once the time came. Then she added hurriedly, "Anyway, it's best to not let a magical object like this out into the world—what if some kid came in here tomorrow and ate one of them?"

"If they had the same effects as they do on your Grandmother, then Becky would have quite the story time." The smile fell away from his face. "April..." he trailed off. Finally he tried to smile again, but it didn't reach his eyes. "Have a good night."

He turned away to go back to whatever he'd been doing.

"Dorian, wait."

It took her a moment to realize the words had actually come out of her mouth. He turned around, an apprehensive look on his face.

"Yes?"

She hesitated only a moment, then stepped across the room, and pressed her mouth against his. His lips didn't taste of fire, like the genie's, but they were warm and soft and entirely human.

His body stiffened. He tried to pull away, but he stood with a table behind him, and it impeded his progress. She moved closer, so close she felt his heartbeat quicken through his layers of clothing—or maybe that was her own heart.

He placed his hands on her shoulders, and pushed her away before he broke the kiss.

She looked down, preparing for his admonishment. He'd made it clear that however strong his attraction to her was, they couldn't act on it. Embarrassment flooded her system, all but dousing the excitement she'd felt moments before.

"April... we..."

"You almost died tonight, Dorian. *We* almost died. I spent a lot of time confused and pissed off that I never got a chance to say how I felt. That wasn't entirely fair, because I didn't *know* how I felt. But today, when I thought you'd died... *really* died..." She trailed off. "You're right. I shouldn't have done this."

She turned to grab her keys off of the table where she'd dropped them, her cheeks burning. Why did she keep making the same dumb mistakes?

He gripped her shoulders firmly, stopping her from going. She didn't struggle, only settled into the shame. "Don't be sorry," he said. He'd meant it in a brotherly way, but then his hands slid down her arms slowly, sending shivers up her spine. His fingers traced the length of hers, and he lightly tapped her fingernails. He looked up, and she froze under his gaze.

He held the back of his hand to her cheek, and then he flipped it around so that it was caressing her face.

"Oh, damn it." His hands fell to her waist, and he pressed his mouth against hers, his curls tickling her cheeks. He pressed towards her, accidentally pulling one of the wooden chairs with him. It squeaked against the floor, and it was her turn to be pushed up against a table.

You just finished *Bookburner,* **the fifth book in the library gate series...**
Since you enjoyed the worlds of the library gate enough to get this far, click
here[1] to sign up for my reader group.
You'll get **free stories** and **sales alerts,** plus book recommendations.
You'll also **be the first to know when the next book is coming out.**
See you there!
-H.
http://www.hdukeauthor.com

---

1. http://www.hdukeauthor.com

More Books by H. Duke

Jeremiah Jones Cowboy Sorcerer Series

Season One Episode Zero: The Key Without a Door (reader group exclusive)

Jeremiah Jones Cowboy Sorcerer: The Complete First Season[1]

Season One Episode One[2]

Season One Episode Two[3]

Season One Episode Three[4]

Season One Episode Four[5]

Season One Episode Five[6]

Season One Episode Six[7]

Season One Episode Seven[8]

Season One Episode Eight[9]

*A Cowboy Sorcerer Christmas (*reader group exclusive*)*

*Taming the Wolf (*reader group exclusive*)*

The Library Gate Series

Pagewalker[10]

Spinebreaker[11]

Wordeater[12]

Inkcaster[13]

Bookburner

---

1. *https://amzn.to/2lHs6kU*

2. *https://amzn.to/2KuHQlT*

3. *https://amzn.to/2KuHQlT*

4. *https://amzn.to/2KuHQlT*

5. *https://amzn.to/2KuHQlT*

6. *https://amzn.to/2KuHQlT*

7. *https://amzn.to/2KuHQlT*

8. *https://amzn.to/2KuHQlT*

9. *https://amzn.to/2KuHQlT*

10. *https://amzn.to/2IB0APa*

11. *https://amzn.to/2KxdNu0*

12. *https://amzn.to/2IAEe0f*

13. *http://hdukeauthor.com/inkcaster*

The First Adventure of Braddy Evers (reader group exclusive)
More books in the Library Gate Series[14]
Horror Books by H. Duke
Things on the Shelf: Three Tales of Christmas Terror[15]
Things on the Shelf 2: More Tales of Holiday Horror[16]
More books in the Holiday Horrors Series[17]
I release new books monthly, so the above list is likely out of date. Find an up-to-date list here.[18]

About H. Duke

H. Duke writes fantasy, horror, and more. She's published over fifteen works of fiction, including the weird west serial *Jeremiah Jones Cowboy Sorcerer,* the Library Gate fantasy portal series, and the Holiday Horror anthology books. These days, she can be seen travelling the United States in her travel trailer with her husband Giru and a shiny black dog named Jupiter. To see an up-to-date list of her works and find out where she'll be writing next, visit *http://www.hdukeauthor.com.*

Table of Contents

Copyright info

---

1. http://www.hdukeauthor.com

www.ingramcontent.com/pod-product-compliance
Lightning Source LLC
Chambersburg PA
CBHW032142170626
46808CB00006B/2341